Harry Dickson

THE AMERICAN SHERLOCK HOLMES
The Werewolf of
Rutherford Grange

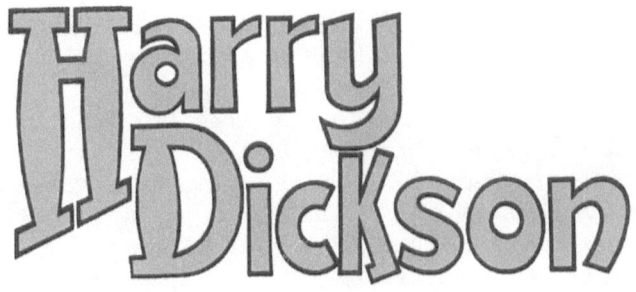

THE AMERICAN SHERLOCK HOLMES

The Werewolf of
Rutherford Grange

and other stories

by
G. L. Gick

A Black Coat Press Book

Visit our website at www.blackcoatpress.com

ISBN 978-1-935558-80-4. First Printing. February 2011. Published by Black Coat Press, an imprint of Hollywood Comics.com, LLC, P.O. Box 17270, Encino, CA 91416. All rights reserved. Except for review purposes, no part of this book may be reproduced or transmitted in any form or by any means, electronic or mechanical, including photocopying, recording, or by any information storage and retrieval system, without permission in writing from the publisher. The stories and characters depicted in this novel are entirely fictional. Printed in the United States of America.

TABLE OF CONTENTS

Foreword

Why pulp?

The question comes into the eyes of my friends; relations; total strangers when they find out what I read most of. Pulp? What's that? 1930s adventure—oh, you mean that Indiana Jones stuff? Who? Doc Savage? Never heard of him. The Shadow…wasn't that some ancient radio show? OK, Sam Spade…Bogie, right? *That* I can understand, but the rest of this stuff…Greg, aren't you a little old to still be reading what's basically prose comic books?

As I write this foreword, in two weeks I will be turning forty-two. F-O-R-T-Y-T-W-O. The answer to Life, the Universe, and Everything, if you believe the late Douglas Adams. Unfortunately, Mr. Adams was wrong—I still don't know how Life, the Universe, and Everything works, and I doubt I'll be finding out at forty-three, forty-four, or at any higher number. But, yeah, on the face of it, I *do* seem to be getting a bit long in the tooth to actually be reading this stuff.

Oh, I've been all over the Pulp map; believe me. I've strolled the 86th Floor with Doc Savage; slunk through dark alleyways with Jimmie Dale and Lamont Cranston; spilled crimson blood with the Spider; fought vampires with Jules de Grandin. I've seen the Maltese Falcon, watched dark R'yleh rise from the deep; found myself trapped in incense-filled dungeons ruled by Fu Manchu. At the movies, I've watched Skull Island go beneath the waves. In the funnies, fought alongside Terry and his Pirate-hunters and hunted tigers with the Phantom. I am on intimate terms with Tarzan, Sherlock Holmes, and Zorro. Non-pulp-wise, I hang out in Narnia and Oz, Mole Hill and the Hundred Acre Wood; travel with the Doctor in the TARDIS; and still visit Calvin and that tiger pal of his whenever I can.

So…why? And why pulp, especially?

The only answer I can really give is…Why Not?

There's a problem with living in the Real World, and it is simply that you eventually get used to it. And in doing so, you tend stop noticing things. Things like stars. And squirrels. And strawberry shakes. Not that your eyes don't register them; of course they do. But you don't really *see* them anymore. Not like you did when you were ten, and the world was a great, mysterious map before you.

I think there's something disappearing in the world today, and that thing is the Sense of Wonder. It still exists, but it seems to be shrinking with each passing year. As our globe becomes smaller, and our civilizations turn into a generic mass called McWorld; we seem to be losing that sense that the world really is an incredible place; a feeling that anything and everything might happen in it. Back in the early 20th Century, when superhighways weren't cutting through the Amazon rain forest and you couldn't find a Burger King in Arabia, that feeling was still there. The world—the universe—was still a big place.

Nowadays, of course, we know there aren't any lost cities out there. We know there aren't any giant apes, or surviving dinosaur islands. We know that we aren't going to hop the rocket to Ganymede with our Martian pen pal anytime in the next few decades; and indeed, there's a good question whether we'll even still *be* here by the end of this century. And I think it's hurt us as humans. I think it's taken something precious away from our psyche—the ability to look at the next hill and ask, *"What's over there?"*

So that's why I read, and write, pulp. It's my way of peeking over that hill, even if I know that nothing's going to be there but a Super Wal-Mart. For a while, at least, I can say: Hey. Somewhere in the world maybe, just maybe, there really is a lost realm of Incas with millions of dollars in gold just lying around. Maybe I really could go to a prehistoric Mars and marry a gorgeous space princess. If not in reality, then at least in the corners of my mind.

And then, maybe, just maybe, I'll take another look at that squirrel running up the tree and see, actually *see*, just what a wonder of Nature it really is. Perhaps not as cool as a living T-Rex, but still an amazing creature in its own way.

Maybe I'll start feeling the cool smoothness of that strawberry shake slide down my throat, and actually appreciate the wonder of its taste.

Maybe I can look at the most mundane aspects of everyday life—and suddenly see the adventure that lies waiting somewhere deep within.

That's why I read pulp. That's why I write it.

And that's why I love it.

Gregory L. Gick

The Werewolf of Rutherford Grange
A Young Harry Dickson adventure

CHAPTER ONE

The Journal of Harrison Dickson, April 1944

Looking back, I am glad I never entrusted this tale to paper before now.

Frankly, I've spent most of my adult life trying to forget it. But, after our recent experience against the Germans with that mysterious French Duke and his allies, Tom Wills had issue to take me aside and ask me again whether, after all we've encountered over the years, I've ever really believed in such a thing as the *supernatural.*

I looked at this young man I had once taken under my wing, now with a family and agency of his own, and had to reply I still just didn't know.

And it is that not knowing that makes me so uncomfortable.

My name is Harry Dickson. I am a private detective by trade, although I have considered myself retired for several years now. If I keep my hand in at all, it is for my own amusement or by the request of the Government, as in my recent case mentioned above. Nonetheless I am glad to say I have had some little success in my chosen career, to the extent that the British press once dubbed me "the American Sherlock Holmes."

Once I might have been proud of the moniker. But, as the years go by, I find the title more and more noisome. While I was indeed born in America, I have not set foot in the country of my birth in years. I was educated in Britain, live in Britain and, in all ways, view myself as a full citizen of that Sceptered Isle. I enjoy regular tea-times, speak with an Oxford accent (put on, I admit, at first, but now such a part of me I cannot speak "normally" without it), and am far more concerned about my local MP than who the President is. No, British I am and British I will be until the end of my days. To call me American does me a disservice.

But further, the title is an offense against my mentor. To even *begin* to consider myself an equal to the Master Detective, who so kindly took an interest in me and guided my early career despite my arrogance and youth, is an affront I would never dare to take. Even S.P.—admittedly an even more dedicated student of the Master than I was, and a man with whom I have never gotten along—would balk at such. I owe the Master nothing less than my training, career, and whatever little fame I may have achieved. I will not tolerate the lowering of his genius so someone as unworthy as I can be placed above him.

Not that many of my adventures over the years wouldn't have caused him to raise his eyebrows in disbelief. Professor Flax. Cric-Croc. Gurrhu and the Temple of Iron. Strange cases, with even stranger criminals. But in just about every instance, even when I was fighting self-styled Babylonian "gods," in the end, I discovered a motive and an explanation that, while perhaps sometimes stretching the boundaries of the laws of science, nevertheless did not break them.

But then, there was *the* case, so early in my career. Just as my mentor had *the* woman, so I have *the* case.

For years, I have kept the incident to the back of my mind. But now, all these years later, I am forced to put it to paper, to try, one last time, to make sense of it all. I doubt I shall. That is why, when this is over, I shall place this manuscript into a safe-deposit box I have rented and promptly try to forget it ever existed. For of all my adventures, this is the one that disturbed me the most. The adventures where I learned that perhaps, just perhaps, there were things in this world hat could not be explained by Rationality alone. The adventure where I met the man who, while never my mentor and perhaps not even my friend, gave me my first glimpse into a world that, despite my best efforts, I still cannot explain.

It was the summer of 1911. King George V had just ascended the throne. The House of Lords would soon give up its power of veto, making the House of Commons dominant in Parliament. The White Star shipping lines were putting the finishing touches on a new ship called the *Titanic*, offering a sparkling new future in comfort and speed on the oceans. And in a tiny room in London, a crass youth of 21 named Harry Dickson had just completed his third year at university, and was preparing to go to work.

Oh, he was an impatient, arrogant youth, this young Dickson. Full of himself and his dreams of the future. True, such could be said of any young person in any era. But this young man particularly thought the world was his for the taking. And why shouldn't he—I—have? For unlike so many of those other youths, my path was already set. I was going to become a private detective, and a great one. Oh, yes. There was no doubt of it. Like my fellow countryman Sherman, my march was inexorable. Had I not already a dozen cases to my credit? Small cases, true; amateur cases, but each brought to a successful conclusion, and by none other than myself. Had I not met and worked with the Master Detective, who pronounced me "promising" and become my guide into the world of detection? Had I not, through his offices, met several others famed in the same line of work—Triggs, Hewitt, the late Mrs. Dene, that unassuming country priest—and had not each one declared me the same? There could be no veering from the path. Like the Ten Commandments, my future was set in stone. I was going to be a detective.

But first, this brash, impertinent youth was informed, he would have to pay his dues.

It seemed my mentor was concerned with me. I was "promising," yes, but in his view far too tempestuous and impatient to strike out on my own just yet. The art of criminal detection was an exacting one, demanding great sacrifices in time and attention, he said. But I was obviously still under the impression most cases a detective handled were like those his chronicler had so romantically exaggerated in *The Strand* when nothing, he said, could be further from the truth.

Detectives had bills to pay just like everyone else, he informed me, and competition was fierce. For every mystery involving red-haired men and orange pips, there were ten cases accepted solely to put bread on the table and a fire in the hearth. Even in the early days before he had made his name, my mentor explained sternly, he had been forced to take whatever he could get to keep the money coming in. Minor matters of blackmail. Dull divorce investigations. Even simply looking into the prospects of a would-be suitor. What I needed, the Master said, was a lesson in the true day-to-day drudgery and ennui most cases actually consisted of. And so he had arranged for me to spend my summer serving an apprenticeship with a Mr. Blake.

I had felt quite elated, at first. Not about the lecture, which I heard rather than listened to, but rather the fact I was to work with Mr. Blake. He was second only to the Master in fame and talent, and would prove to be one of the kindest and most encouraging of men. Looking back, I find that I did indeed learn much from him. But he had listened to the Master more closely than I, and, as a consequence, my apprenticeship to him was, as my countrymen might say, "dull as watching paint dry."

The stipulation of my working with Mr. Blake was simple: at no time was I to be permitted to work directly on a case of any import. I was solely to be used to assist in gathering whatever background research he might need, or to do legwork in whatever small, negligible cases Mr. Blake might have accepted to pass the time in between his major affairs. And so for the past two months I had spent most of my time muddling through dusty old books in the British Museum or engaged in chemical experiments while Blake was off on his own adventures. While he fought a notorious Devil Doctor in Limehouse, I examined mushy fingerprints gathered after a clumsy burglary. While he sloshed through the sewers of Paris searching for the secret hideout of a black-coated conspiracy, I followed a husband through the seedier parts of Soho to see which brothels he frequented. While Blake hung upside-down trying to free himself from a runaway balloon, I spent long hours searching through Burke's *Peerage* to discover the supposed birthright of an obscure chimney sweep. I also fed and walked the dog.

It was incredibly frustrating. One of the most promising (that word again) would-be investigators of the 20th century, and here I was wasting my talents on discovering the potential spousal possibilities of the local butcher instead of being on the scene of master crimes looking for clues. And, although I never said as such, my feelings were obvious to all who worked with me.

This particular day, however, I was in rather high spirits. It was a pleasant summer morning. The sun was out, the sky a deep sapphire blue, and I decided to forego the expense of a cab in order to walk to work. Mr. Blake had just praised me the other day for some research I had done on the secret meanings of Celtic knot work, which had happily cracked a puzzling case for him. Implicit within his words was the possibility that I should be rewarded for it somehow. My youthful mind filled itself with fantasies of what it might prove to be: a raise? A real case? Dare I say—a *partnership?* Mature as I liked to think myself, I practically skipped across the pavement at the thought.

I saw only one thing that disturbed my bonhomie: in a storefront, someone had placed the sign: "Dr. Tin Zen: Spiritualist—Make Contact with Your Loved Ones Beyond the Veil! Prices negotiable." Beneath was a picture of a fat, balding, middle-aged "Chinese" man— obviously a Caucasian in makeup—hovering with what he evidently thought of as a "mysterious" air over a crystal ball. Rather, as he loomed over the orb, it seemed as though his tonnage was about to topple him right on top of the thing.

I sighed and shook my head. To begin with, Tin Zen was a ridiculous name. No self-respecting real Chinaman would possess such an alias. But my antipathy stemmed from more than that. I regarded the very premise of Spiritualism with a deep, abiding loathing; as I might a child beater or a dead rat.

I have never been a religious man. If asked at what altar I primarily worship, I would have answered at only two: those of the Twin Idols of Logic and Reasoning. It was a legacy from my mentor. Everything could be explained if one simply used his rationality, he informed me once; there was no such thing as magic to a true detective. So you may imagine that the very idea that gazing cross-eyed into a crystal ball could somehow call up the spirit of your deceased Uncle Charlie, who would then tell you the secrets of Heaven in such a vague, nondescript way that you were even more puzzled when you went out than when you came, was anathema to me. But what appalled me most was how many otherwise normal, intelligent people believed in it. I had seen them: men and women, smiling indulgently at the thought of life on Mars; laughing aloud at anyone who claimed to see a sea serpent. But then those very same would spend hours clutching each others' hands in a darkened room looking for the ectoplasmic halo of their dead mother.

Perhaps I should not have been so biting toward people who simply wanted to see their loved ones again, but there it was. Even had I not been the son of a famed stage magician, I had seen all the tricks mediums used to fake "spirits" performed a hundred times. I knew them to be nothing more than illusions, and in my mind expected the same from everyone else.

Ah, well. If the foolish and gullible had nothing else better to do with their money, then so be it. I had my own future to consider. With the promise of upcoming reward for my services, nothing was about to destroy my mood this day. After all, I thought, whatever it might be could hardly be duller than my currently duties!

So you may understand my surprise when I walked in to a chorus of angry voices issuing out of Blake's private office.

"Damn it all, Blake, I don't want one of your wretched men! I want you!"

"Sir Henry, I already told you—"

"I don't care what you told me!"

I looked inquiringly over at Tinker, Blake's full-time assistant, sitting at his desk. He waved me to silence, a look of consternation upon his face. From behind the door, I could hear the patient voice of the detective himself:

"Sir Henry, I'm afraid it's impossible for me to personally come to your home at this time. I'm already deeply involved in another case, and it looks as though the trail is leading to Geneva. I may have to leave for the continent at any moment. I simply cannot break away. My men are perfectly capable—"

The first voice, loud and tinged with arrogance: "If I wanted a second-rate constable in charge of this, Blake, I would have hired one. This conference is too important to my fu—to the future of England to trust to inferiors, and I promised the attendees a top man to ensure its safety!"

A third voice, much younger and quieter, but stiff: "Mr. Blake, perhaps you don't comprehend the situation here. Security is of great importance to this conference, and—"

Mr. Blake's voice again, sounding very patient: "I comprehend the situation perfectly, Mr. Westenra. But as I understand it, your father has already hired agents from eight firms to help provide security. I know these men and they are all quite competent. Surely you do not need—"

"None of them are as good as you, Blake!" snarled the first voice.

"I appreciate the compliment, sir, but—"

"I never make compliments," thundered the speaker. "I only speak facts. And in your case, that's little enough, Blake. I don't believe in half the nonsense published about you. But you owe me, and—"

As the argument, whatever it was about, continued to rage, Blake's assistant and I exchanged looks, then shrugged. I took out my pipe and began to light it. As I did, the door to Mr. Blake's office opened and his dark, handsome face peered out.

"Ah, Master Dickson!" There was a smile on his face, but the cheerful tone behind it seemed distinctly false. "Good to see you! Would you be so kind as to step into my office a moment?"

I felt a sudden sinking sensation. I glanced back toward Tinker, who shrugged again, but with the thinnest of smiles. *Better you than I*, his expression clearly read. But there was nothing else for it, so I put out my pipe, obediently chimed, "Yes, sir," and went inside.

I had always admired Mr. Blake's office. I wished for one just like it when I got out on my own. It was sumptuous, yet comfortable, with fine leather-backed chairs and an expensive mahogany desk. The walls were lined with bookcases, save for behind the desk, which was a full plate-glass window, offering him a fine view of the comings and goings of Baker Street. It was also unnaturally crowded. In addition to Mr. Blake and myself, two others stood in the room.

The eldest stood fuming before Blake's desk, literally, as clenched in his mouth was a large, ill-smelling cigar. He was probably somewhere in his early sixties, and his hair and thick mustache were dappled grey. His frame was actually relatively lengthy, but with a hefty paunch distorting and bloating outward from his otherwise expertly-tailored clothing, he appeared much shorter than he should have. His skin was florid and beaded with perspiration even in the relatively cool room. Black eyes snapped arrogantly at my employer through a pair of expensive but slightly cockeyed spectacles. Looking at him, I was reminded of nothing so much as a caricature of G.K. Chesterton out of *Punch*—but without the natural *bon homine* of that celebrated writer.

The second man was much younger, perhaps 26 or so. He hung back in one of the corners, arms folded, seemingly quite bored with the proceedings. Unlike his companion he was handsome; with dark eyes, a firm, strong chin, and a thin, straight nose, but it was a chilly, unemotional attractiveness. Compared to his elder—who was at least active, for all his girth—this man was a contemptuous mannequin. He had a queer little smile on his face, like someone who knew a great joke he was playing on all the world, and they simply couldn't recognize it.

But now Mr. Blake was speaking: "Dickson, may I present Sir Henry Westenra and his son, Alexander. Gentlemen, my employee, Harry Dickson."

"Gentlemen." I bowed slightly and proffered my hand. They stared at me. I looked back and forth, from one to another. Neither moved. I lowered my hand.

"No," Sir Henry barked. "No, no, no, no, no, no, no. He won't do at all. Boy's barely out of short pants. What are you trying to hand me, Blake?" He glared at my employer, as if daring him to speak

Mr. Blake closed his eyes and sighed, very low and long. "Mr. Dickson is perfectly capable of handling the requirements of your situation, Sir Henry. He has worked for me and several other detectives, and we find him most promising."

"That would be fine," bristled Westenra, "if I wanted someone *promising*. I want someone *competent*, Blake, with experience." Suddenly he wheeled toward me. "You, boy. Where'd you go to school?"

"I've just completed my third year at South Kensington, sir."

"Kensington?" Alexander Westenra, the mannequin, spoke for the first time. I was amazed his lips could move. "Isn't that the school Geoffrey Rutherford attended?"

Immediately, Sir Henry snorted derisively and raised his eyes to heaven. "The Rutherfords," he spat contemptuously. "Don't even speak to me about the Rutherfords."

"Well, it's not Christina's fault Peter made such a hash of things," Alexander replied calmly. "She's not responsible for him being what he is." Suddenly, he smiled wickedly. "Besides, look at it this way—at least now we can be sure your grandchildren won't howl."

"Enough, I say! Damn it all, Blake!" Sir Henry twisted back toward my employer. "I don't want children! I want *you!* Now are you coming or aren't you?"

"No, Sir Henry," Blake said through gritted teeth. "I am not." He strode to his desk and sat. "For the last time. I am deeply involved in another case the Prime Minister himself asked me to look into I cannot—*cannot*—break away right now. Either you take Mr. Dickson, or you take nothing. Or would you rather take it up with Mr. Asquith himself?" He lifted the phone receiver. "I can ring him up, at any moment. Now, what's it going to be?"

For a long moment, Westenra stared at Blake, eyes boggling as if they was about to burst His head twisted toward me sharply, glared me up and down, and finally snarled: "All right, Blake. I'll take him. But he'll have to remember just who is in charge. The slightest mistake and he's out. And mind you—if that happens, I'll make certain everyone knows he's your employee!"

He whipped around quickly for such a fat man and stalked toward the door. Over his shoulder, he called: "I'll expect you by two o'clock tomorrow afternoon, young man! I'll have someone waiting at the station to pick you up! See that you're not late! Come along, Alexander!"

With a flourish, he threw open the door and left. Alexander Westenra, after a cold nod to each of us, followed. A moment later, we heard the door to the street fling open and slam shut.

Mr. Blake sank his head to his desk with a groan. "That," he said, "was Sir Henry Westenra."

"So I gathered," I replied wryly.

Blake sighed. "Don't be impertinent, Dickson; it doesn't suit you. Do you know anything about him?"

"No, sir."

"Well, you're about to learn. Sit."

I did so. He spun his own chair around to face the window, steepling his fingers together thoughtfully "Sir Henry Westenra has come to that title only five years ago, when he was granted it due to his work in India. At least, that is the story; in point of fact, he received it due to nepotism and his one great talent, as you will see While up until now his family have never been granted titles or peerages, they're extremely rich and influential—they're apparently distantly related to the Westenras of Whitby, whom you may have heard of—and are based in a remarkably ugly domicile in Surrey he had constructed with his late wife's money—not his—and called, with all due modesty, Westenra House." Mr. Blake turned to face me, a little smile playing across his lips. "Are you with me so far?" I nodded.

"Good. Now. The Westenras have always had interests in India; apparently quite a bit of their money is invested there. As a result, the sons of the Westenras have, as a rule, entered either the Army or the Foreign Office, specializing in the subcontinent. Henry Westenra was the latest to do so. He became a small functionary in the Office, and was based, I believe, in Bombay. There he married—very late, and to a very rich woman—and had two sons; Alexander, whom you met, and Peter, the youngest. Still, nothing much was expected of him. It is well known that Sir Henry is not the brightest light in the Office." Mr. Blake turned back toward the window, thoughtfully. "However, this is where it all matters. For all his incompetence—and he is *very* incompetent from what I've heard—Sir Henry Westenra has one great ability. He is very, very good at being in the right place at the right time.

"What happened was this. There was what appeared to be a small uprising in Bombay A group of native Muslims had walked into a small white community, and Sir Henry just *happened* to be on the scene when it occurred. He managed to escape, get the Army and lead them back, where the 'uprising' was put down in a most bloody manner." He sighed. "As it turned out, the natives were there to protest the mistreatment of their women by certain British officials. Among them, it seems, Westenra's son Alexander. They had no intention of doing violence; they simply wanted to lodge their protests with the local officials. There were no survivors."

For a moment, Mr. Blake simply sat silently. Then: "The whole affair was hushed up, of course. No questions were asked. Natives vanish in India all the time, I'm told. If not addressed, no one cares. But some of Westenra's relatives higher up in the Office heard about their scion's 'heroics,' and insisted he receive some kind of reward. They made such a fuss that to finally shut them up, Sir Henry was granted his knighthood and has used it to advance his career ever since. Two years ago, he was recalled to England, and now works directly for the Office. Which brings me to why he was here today."

Mr. Blake leaned towards me intently. "You need to understand, Dickson. Sir Henry is a fool, an ass and as self-centered a boor as I've ever had the misfortune to meet. But he knows where to be and when, and he knows how to curry favors and when to call them in. As a result, he has made himself look far more important to the outside world than he actually is. And there are a great deal of important people who are in his debt. Myself, unfortunately, being one of them."

He pulled out his pipe and lit it, indicating that I could do the same. I was grateful for the opportunity. I had the sensation the next few words were not going to be something I would enjoy hearing.

"Two years ago, while working on a case, I was obliged to go to Sir Henry for some information the Office had on a certain suspect," Blake said quietly. "The information was very sensitive, and something I should not have had, but without it a dangerous murderer would've escaped the gallows. Sir Henry gave it to me, but with the stipulation that I, as a private investigator, would owe him one favor when he needed it. Yesterday, he called that favor in."

Once again he spun around toward the window. "This weekend, there will be a conference between Great Britain and France. Through his sources, Sir Henry has somehow managed to get permission to host the entire affair at his estate. Why, I do not know, but it undoubtedly involves puffing himself up to his superiors. *Supposedly,* this conference is merely on matters of various economic aspects of our respective colonies, particularly Ceylon and India. You know, discussions of tariffs and such. But I suspect it involves rather more than that. Firstly, a man like Sir Henry does not take an interest in something so mundane as importation fees. Secondly, the main attendee from France will be the Duc d'Origny himself."

I stifled a gasp and nodded. The Duc d'Origny! Although fairly unknown to the general public, even in his own country, the Duc was a near-legend in government circles. In his younger days, he had been a government agent for France, traveling the Far East and South Asia and infiltrating dozens of rebel groups. It was he who had been instrumental in revealing to the West just how fully the fingers of Russian imperialism were spreading in the East and, it was said, had personally stemmed an invasion of Tibet by the Tsar's forces several years earlier. No one knew more about the influence of Moscow in our colonies than he. The Duc was very old now, and had for the most part retired, but he had remained on call in an advisory capacity by his own government—and, on occasion, ours. If he was to be in attendance, then this conference was definitely concerned with anything but tariffs!

"Naturally enough," Mr. Blake was continuing, "such a important conference would need adequate security. And that is why Sir Henry contacted me. He wanted me to take charge of it personally. You saw that I refused—but nevertheless a favor is a favor. Therefore, someone from this office must go in my place. That someone is you, Dickson."

I'm afraid I groaned rather more loudly than I intended. From all that I had heard, I should have expected something like this, but really! Security detail? Mere security detail! And here I had been expecting a reward for good work!

Mr. Blake, seeing the obvious despair upon my face, chuckled, then reached over to pat me consolingly on the shoulder. "Now, now, Dickson, it isn't as bad as all that. It's something every detective has to do now and then. We have to deal with all sorts of people in our trade, and you'll find that very few of them are actually pleasant to work with. Particularly the aristocracy." He smiled briefly. "Do you think this is a punishment, Dickson?"

I coughed, cleared my throat, and started, "Well, sir, I—"

"Well, it isn't," Blake interrupted sternly. "Nothing of the sort. I must admit, I've been very pleased with your work thus far. Like your mentor, for your age I find you very promising. In fact, I was going to recommend to him that I go ahead and place you in full charge of some of my smaller cases to see how you did, but this takes precedence. It'd be good practical experience for you, and you need that. Without such, you can spend your career ratiocinating about murders all you like, and it will make not one whit of difference to you as a detective." He picked up a pen and fiddled with it. "It's only for half-a-week, Dickson. Besides, you'll be in a position of more responsibility than you think. With Westenra 'taking charge' of things himself since I'm not there, he's bound to make a mess of it, and I'll need you to help keep things on an even keel. The other agents he'll have there are good-hearted chaps but rather vacuous, so try to keep an eye on him and guide him as best you can. Besides, before the conference you might even get some time to go sightseeing. I hear the countryside's quite beautiful. Very steeped in folklore and occult history, too, I understand. Are you at all interested in the occult, Dickson?"

"No, sir," I replied honestly. "I have no belief in the supernatural in the least. The Master once told me that when it comes to the rational mind, no ghosts need apply. I have never seen any reason to disregard that advice."

"Hmmm," Blake murmured thoughtfully. "He would say that. Never likes to admit anything outside his precious ratiocination skills. One day I should tell you what he and I encountered once in the catacombs under Bayonne. But that's neither here nor there. You'll find some notes on the Westenras and their guests upon your desk, Dickson. After you walk Pedro, I suggest you spend the rest of the day studying it. You leave first thing tomorrow morning."

He glanced up at the clock in the corner. "And I have to get busy. I'm lunching with the Becks today, and have to get this paperwork finished. Dismissed."

There was nothing else left to say. Feeling a great weight on my shoulders, I stood to go. Then I thought of something. "Sir?"

"Yes?"

"Excuse me, but you told Sir Henry that the Prime Minister might have you leave for Geneva at any moment. I was unaware he had retained you for any case."

"Oh, that," Blake smiled. "I'm sorry, Dickson. I lied. If I had gone to Westenra House, I should have throttled the man before the weekend was out. Never could stand him. You know how it is—Rank Has Its Privileges and all that."

Then he smiled broadly. "Cheer up, Dickson! As I said, it's only for a couple of days! Besides, it's *Surrey,* for God's sake! What could possibly happen there?"

CHAPTER TWO

Despite my disappointment, never let it be said a Dickson ever shirked his duty. I arrived at the station bright and early, taking one of the private compartments Mr. Blake had kindly booked for me (Sir Henry having apparently not bothered). I had brought with me the file I had been given, and while the train was beginning to pull out, I opened it to reacquaint myself with its contents.

There was little about Sir Henry I did not already know, save that his wife had passed on a few years earlier. Currently he lived in his ancestral home, Westenra House, some few miles outside the village of Wolfsbridge. I had never heard of the town in question, figuring it to be the archetypical tiny collection of insular housing seemingly ubiquitous throughout Britain.

Of rather more interest were his two sons, Alexander and Peter. Both were also members of the Foreign Office, albeit at lower levels than their father, and both would be present at the conference. Both had been born in India, although Peter, the youngest by two years, had proven a very frail, sickly child. Photographs of the two showed the waxly handsome Alexander looming over a sallower, thinner young man, with fair hair and pale eyes. There was a quiet sadness about the image of Peter Westenra that caught my attention. Within each picture there was an air about his visage that seemed to read as if he wished to be anywhere else but there, in that illustration, beside his family. Knowing what little I did of them, I found it difficult to blame him. Still, the information about him in the files was scant. Primarily it seemed he did his work quietly, avoided trouble, and had maintained his bachelor status after most men his age were married with families.

Alexander was more intriguing. After Blake's assertion that this Westenra had been considered something of a rake while in India, I found the file added that there were reports of other incidents he had been involved in, which Sir Henry had often been forced to extricate him from. The details were vague, but it was said he was often seen in the company of characters of unsavory repute, and had often been involved with fights with the native population. Since returning to England, however, he had married, maintained a home in London and apparently had calmed his hot temper considerably.

So intent was I on my reading I almost didn't hear the voice ask: "Excuse me, young fellah-me-lad, are these seats taken? It's too noisy in the other cars, and when you've got two ladies wantin' conversation, you have to look elsewhere."

I looked up to see a tall, lean, but well-built man gazing with regal amiableness down at me. He had obviously seen much travel in foreign climes over the years, for his face and hands were bronzed and toughened by storm and sun. He seemed vaguely familiar to me somehow, but I could not place him. Besides, it was his two companions that garnered most of my attention.

Unlike my mentor, I have never been totally... impervious to the presence of the fairer sex. And the two that accompanied this man were fair, indeed. The youngest was a beautiful girl of about 18 years, brandishing a glorious crown of sun-gold hair that seemed to shimmer with every movement. High cheekbones, a pert nose and intense blue eyes completed the ensemble. A lovely picture, indeed, but compared with her companion, still shallow. She was standing behind the others, but was almost as tall as her male associate. Of obvious Mediterranean ancestry, a flowing mane of cascading black hair created an ebon halo around perfect porcelain features that seemed to glow, even in the relatively bright light of the car.

I instantly stood and bowed, more to her than to her companions, although she was clearly my elder by some five or six years. "No—no, not at all," said I, cursing myself for stammering like a schoolboy. "Please, do come in."

They did, the man sitting next to me, the women across. From the look in their eyes, I could see they noticed my attraction and were amused. I flushed, but managed to introduce myself.

The man accepted my hand, shaking it vigorously. "Name's Roxton, youngster," he said, and instantly I realized why he seemed so familiar. There was hardly one in the British Isles who had not heard of the famous aristocrat, hunter and explorer! He was on the level of Burton and Quatermain. He had first made his name with his trip to a fabled South American plateau and his renown had only grown since. He was one of the few white men to have ever penetrated Mecca (in disguise) and had fought pirates in the Malay jungles. He had even (it was said) spent over a year in the desolate Sahara, searching for a legendary lost city supposed to be the last outpost of Atlantis. Seeing he had been recognized, he smiled and indicated his companions: "And may I present Miss Christina Rutherford of Wolfsbridge and Miss Gianetti Annunciata, late of Milan."

And whither are you bound, Mr. Dickson?" Miss Rutherford asked in a charming voice.

My eyes wanted to keep drinking in Miss Annunciata, but it would be impolite to ignore the rest of my company. Besides, Christina Rutherford—hadn't Alexander mentioned a girl by that name? So I answered, and she laughed musically: "Why, Wolfsbridge is where we're heading, too! It's my home. We can all get off together."

"I'm sure that would be delightful, Miss Rutherford," replied I politely.

"Oh, please, call me Christina," Miss Rutherford interjected. "I hate ceremony. Uncle John does, too, but he's old-fashioned when it comes to women."

I saw Lord John look sharply at her, but Miss Rutherford merely stuck out her tongue at him. "Very well, then—Miss Christina," I said.

But for obvious reasons most of my attention was on the lovely Miss Annunciata. So you may imagine my heart trilled more than slightly when she asked in perfect English with just a hint of Mediterranean charm: "And you may call me Gianetti, as well. Or Miss Gianetti, if you must."

"If you'll pardon me, Dickson," Lord John interrupted, obviously wishing to change the subject, "do I hear a slight American accent in your voice?"

"Very likely, sir," I replied. "I am American. But my father wished me to have a British education, so I was schooled here."

"Good decision-makin'," Roxton nodded. "Finest schools in the world here. Where'd you go?"

"Pertwee, sir. I originally intended to attend a place called Brookfield, but circumstances changed that."

"Dickson, Dickson," Miss Gianetti was murmuring. "Would you by chance be related to a detective I've heard of called Allan Dickson? But he's Australian, I believe—perhaps I am incorrect."

I smiled broadly. "Not at all. As a matter of fact, I am related to him. Quite closely. He's myself."

"Oh?"

"Yes. You see, Allan is my middle name. I went by it for a time a few years ago."

"But you're American,"

"True, but that's simple enough to explain. You see, my father was a traveling magician. While touring in Sydney, he met my mother. I picked the accent up from her. When I went to university, I decided to use it again to annoy my Latin professor. He never could tolerate his subject spoken with a Brisbane twang. Like this—*Veni, vidi, vici.*" My tongue slurred with my thickest Antipodean.

Miss Gianetti and Miss Christina laughed, and even Lord John smiled. "So you are a detective, then, Mr. Harry?" Christina asked.

"Well," I squirmed a moment, "not quite. That is, I have yet to start my own practice. But I have been involved in a few cases on an amateur basis. And solved each successfully, I may add." I was bragging, I knew. But then, I was trying to get the attention of two remarkably beautiful women. Still and all,, my conscience did get the better of me, for I added, a bit abashedly: "Truthfully, I'm surprised you have even heard of me at all, Miss Gianetti. 'Allan' Dickson didn't last long."

"Oh," she replied airily, " I wouldn't have, but my guru has a habit of collecting files on unusual crimes. It's one of his hobbies." She smiled pertly, and I felt a bit crushed. Clearly my fame hadn't preceded me as much as I'd hoped.

"Yes, your mysterious teacher," giggled Christina. "When are we going to meet him, Gianetti? Mother invited him, you know."

Gianetti nodded. "I know, but he rarely accepts such invitations anymore. He's much too busy with his own research."

"Research? Researches in what?" I asked automatically. As I did I suddenly felt rather than saw Lord John tense beside me.

"Why, the Spirit World, of course," Miss Gianetti replied as if it were the most natural thing in the world.

What?

I couldn't believe it. I had to be hearing things. Surely, these two lovely, obviously intelligent women, and a famous aristocrat who had seen so much of the world, weren't being serious! Spiritualists! No wonder Roxton had suddenly stiffened. Sadly, I was reminded again of just how pervasive such irrationality had become in the world. If such a man as Lord John Roxton could believe in such nonsense, what chance had I to stop it?

My thoughts must have been plain on my face, for Miss Gianetti said, "Ah. You don't believe in Spiritualism, I take it."

It was too late to turn back now. Truth had forced my hand. "I'm afraid to say I do not, Miss Gianetti. I am a decided Rationalist. I believe in the powers of Science and Reason, not superstition."

"But so do I, Mr. Dickson!" Miss Gianetti leaned forward intently "Very much so! And so does my guru, who taught me so much. It was he who first discovered my potential as a medium, and it was he who taught me how to approach it the way I do—as a Science! He knows very well all the fakery that's out there and despises it. But he also knows that there are some things that cannot be explained by the use of the mind alone, Mr. Dickson. We can only discover so much, because we can only comprehend so much. The rest we have to leave up to faith."

I fear I may have smirked a bit. "Faith, Miss Gianetti?"

"Yes, faith," Miss Christina suddenly chose to put in. "Faith that there's something out there greater than ourselves, and faith that somehow, we continue on after death. You see, my father just recently passed on,"—she fingered her hat wistfully—"and Mother was absolutely devastated. They were so much in love. She has to know that he's all right; that he's in Heaven and happy. So I've gotten a number of mediums, including Gianetti, to come and hold a séance to prove that he's still there; that we don't just turn to dust when we die. We're going to make contact with my father again, Mr. Dickson. And then you'll see the true power of faith."

I coughed uncomfortably. "Be that as it may, Miss Christina, but—"

"Come along, young fellah," Lord John interrupted suddenly, "let's go out and have ourselves a smoke."

"I have cigarettes, Uncle John," Christina protested, reaching for her handbag.

Roxton rolled his eyes as he stood. "Women shouldn't be poisonin' their lungs with such things, Christina."

"Oh, pooh," his niece replied, and to prove her point she lit right up.

Roxton sighed; this was a battle he had obviously fought many times. "This way, Dickson," he said, ushering me out into the train's corridor. Carefully he guided me well down the corridor, out of the slightest possible earshot of the women. Then, gazing at me with iron seriousness, he turned and said to me:

"Young man, I've been to a lot of places in this world and seen a lot of strange things. I've seen creatures in the Matto Grosso that could swallow you whole in one bite, and I've seen a man I examined myself and said was dead rise up again when a Congolese witch doctor got 'hold of him. I'm not sayin' I'm believen' any of this Spiritualist guff myself—not for a moment. But Geoffrey Rutherford was related to a zoologist I've been through a lot with, and ever since she was a child Christina's called me 'Uncle.' But since he died his wife Althea—Christina's mother—has been on the weak side with mournin,' and she's gone from a good church-goin' Christian to becoming obsessed with this Spiritualist ballyhoo. She's got herself convinced she can't get well until she knows Geoffrey's still alive on 'the other side,' y'know? Well, it's gotten to the point that if that's what it take to get her up and around again, I'm goin' to put it with it. You understand?"

"I believe I do, sir. I can well understand the desire to feel a loved one is still somehow present, even after death. But, at the risk of sounding callous, I thought this was where this much-vaunted 'faith' spoke of came in. That a true believer in the survival of the soul would not *need* proof that life was somehow eternal."

Roxton smiled. "You might be righter than you know, young fellah. Nonetheless, Althea is convinced the only way to assure herself of Geoffrey's continued existence is through this séance, and I'm beginning to think Christina has, as well. But I must ask you to not involve yourself in this. I know what kind of hoaxin' these 'mediums' are into. Let me handle it."

After a moment, I nodded. "As you say, your lordship," I said. "But if I may, what about Miss Annunciata?"

"She's a very beautiful and charmin' woman."

"A fraud, of course."

"Of course. But a most attractive fraud."

" Miss Christina seems very fond of her."

"That she is. Christina has a knack of making friends instantly. But I have to admit, the odd thing about Miss Annunicata is that I get a strange feelin' she's bein' honest about herself. Let me explain. It is almost as if—well—as if she honestly and genuinely believes she *is* a medium of some kind, instead of engaging in open chicanery. Oh, I'm not saying she's mad. Far from it. But I think we both know that delusions can run deep. I have to wonder if this mysterious 'teacher' of hers isn't some sort of second Svengali, tricking her for his own ends. Too bad he is not coming. I would rather like to find out—for her sake."

There was nothing to say to that. We smoked, then returned to our compartment to find the ladies waiting, apparently having finished their own cigarettes. Gianetti gaze upon me was calm. Clearly she had guessed what we had been talking about, but decided to say nothing. Instead, she merely asked: "And why are you going to Wolfsbridge, Mr. Dickson?"

"Just to do some research for my employer," I lied carefully. Seeing as the conference was supposed to be so sensitive, early on I had decided not to tell anyone my business.

"Oh," replied Christina, "you mean you're going to Sir Henry's silly meeting."

My thoughts must have clearly showed, for the girl burst out laughing. "Oh, Mr. Dickson, *everyone* in town knows about this big secret conference!" she chortled. "Sir Henry's done nothing but brag about it for months! The man's such a pompous ass! He just loves to show how much more important he is than we lowly serfs! And Alexander's exactly the same way. It's Peter I feel sorry for—he's so sweet, and they treat him so badly. Especially after Sir Henry tried to get us—"

"Christina, don't tell stories," Roxton said sternly.

"Oh, all right," Christina sighed, "But it's a shame about Peter. He's such a dear man."

"Yes," replied Lord John, "but that's enough."

I decided it was time to change the subject. I had no wish to speak of the Westenras, the conference, or Spiritualism any longer. So I instead turned the discussion to some of Lord John's previous adventures, of which he was more than willing to elaborate upon. Despite my doubts of her, Miss Gianetti proved both fascinated and fascinating, and so the rest of our journey passed in a most pleasurable fashion.

I was pleasantly surprised to find the town of Wolfsbridge much livelier and bustling than I had anticipated. I was expecting a tiny, rather insular village; what I received was a fair-sized market town, with busy streets and shops, paved roads, a telephone and telegraph line, and even cars roaring through town. Who knew—there might even be a building with indoor plumbing! I had taken Miss Gianetti's bag; Lord John had Christina's, and we had just stepped off the train. Miss Christina's expression was one of happiness in familiar surroundings and we set off to look for her mother, whom Christina had stated would be there to greet them.

As we did, a particular feature caught my eye and held it. A small, pale-white stone bridge, arching over the small rivulet that passed through town. Unlike the rest of the architecture, which was typically Tudor, there was something distinctly Mediterranean about the bridge, with its ionic columns rising from the water and the faded images of nymphs and fauns carved in its sides. Someone had taken much time and care to build it many, many years ago. Miss Christina had followed my eyes and nodded. "Yes, it's the oldest thing in the village. Dates back to Roman times, I've heard. Isn't it beautiful?"

"It is," I said. "And that's obviously the 'bridge' part of 'Wolfsbridge.' But the 'Wolf' half?"

"Oh. Well, that's rather difficult to explain. But there's Mother; do come and meet her!" And ere I could protest, the young lady had seized my elbow and was propelling me eagerly forward.

At the edge of the station, a long white motorcar stood waiting by the kerb, engine running. The driver stood smartly beside the door, while resting in the back seat waited a woman. "Mama!" Christina called out, steering us toward her

"Christina, my dear." She raised herself up eagerly enough to meet her daughter's kiss, but it was clear it was an effort for her. Mrs. Althea Rutherford was still a comparatively young woman, somewhere in her late forties, and still bore the hallmarks of a youthful great beauty. She possessed her daughter's hair and coloring, and, as maturity had set in, her features had grown more and more dignified. She looked, to me, like the queen one might expect a princess to become in a fairy tale after Prince Charming whisked her away; balancing regality, compassion, and just a slight hint of mischief in her eyes.

But since her husband's death that appearance had grown drawn and sallow; and she lay in the back seat with a blanket over her as if she might catch a chill even in the summer air. "I do hope you didn't pick up any of those awful cigarettes in London, my dear," Mrs. Rutherford was saying. "You know how your father disapproved of women who smoked."

"Of course not, Mama," Christina said cheerfully. "Everyone knows a real lady wouldn't poison her lungs with such things." She shot a mischievous glance over at Roxton, but the latter wisely ignored it. Instead, he bent to kiss Mrs. Rutherford's hand and say, "Althea It's truly wonderful to see you up and around again. We were all so concerned."

"Thank you, John. But nothing will be right until I can speak with dear Geoffrey again."

"That's what we're trying to do, Mama," Christina interrupted, reaching out to take Gianetti's hand. "This is Miss Annunciata, the assistant of the Sâr Dubnotal. She's going to help us, just like you asked."

"It's a pleasure to meet you, Mrs. Rutherford," Gianetti spoke softly, taking the elder woman's other hand. "And I hope I can help. I know well the pain left behind when a loved one crosses the veil."

"Oh my dear, I do hope so. I miss him so much."

"We'll try. It's much harder to contact, truly contact, the deceased than one might think. But keep faith— for faith is power, and love is the strongest faith of all. We'll find him. Now—you said in your letter than you had contacted other mediums as well as the Doctor? Are they here yet?"

"No; they'll be arriving tomorrow. Rosemary Underwood, who is a local medium everyone tells me is excellent, and a very, very famous psychic from Russia, Count Gregori Yeltsin. Do you know him?"

"Yeltsin?" Gianetti frowned thoughtfully. "No, I'm afraid not. Which is odd—*El Tebib* makes it a point to keep up with any mediums operating out of Russia. He's never spoken of any named Yeltsin."

"Really? He's reputed to be an associate of Blavatsky, and to have studied under the Hidden Masters in Tibet."

This was too much for me. "If I may, Miss Gianetti," I put in, "just *why* does your employer go out of his way to keep track of Russian mediums?"

Everyone's attention was now turned to me. "Mama, this is Mr. Dickson," Christina introduced me. "He was on the train with us. And guess what, he attends Papa's old school! He's a detective, and is going to be working security at that conference Sir Henry is holding this weekend."

"Really?" She smiled weakly but with genuine warmth. "My dear young man, words cannot express how sorry I am for you. I'm afraid you're in for quite a time."

I chuckled a bit and bowed. "Thank you, Ma'am. But, if you please, Miss Gianetti, if I may, just who *is* this employer of yours? What does he do for a living? What did you call him again—Sir Dubnose?"

Miss Gianetti burst out laughing. "Oh, how he'd scream if he heard you call him that! No, no—the *Sâr Dubnotal*, although he prefers to be called *El Tebib* or simply the Doctor. He's... he's... well, it's hard to explain just *what* he is. I suppose the best way to describe him is as an explorer."

"Like His Lordship?"

"Not quite. Lord John, bless you, sir, only explores *physical* realms. *El Tebib* studies more than that. His explorations are those of the higher planes; of the *psychognosis*. The realm of the powers of the mind and spirit; of the mysteries of life and what lies beyond."

I was confused. "He's an alienist, then?"

"No, not exactly, although you could call him one. The Doctor explores the hidden recesses of the mind, yes, but also that of the soul, of the powers and secrets we all have within us. But to find those secrets, we sometimes have to reach beyond life, to those who have already passed on. I merely use my small abilities to assist in his research. But we both use our knowledge for the betterment of others. As for his interest in Russia—well, let us just say there are those who seek the same secrets, but for their own purposes. The Doctor doesn't approve of that."

"I see," I said, and felt disappointed. So this "Sâr Dubnotal" was simply some sort of would-be occultist. Another Spiritualist who thought they could find all the answers to life's problems from the dead. Lord John sidled up to me and whispered in my ear. "I've heard of him. Some Frenchman who visited India and went a bit native, or so they say. Probably just as much a fraud as the rest, but that's my concern."

"Would you care to attend the séance with us, Mr. Dickson?" Mrs. Rutherford asked. "It's not until this Friday."

I coughed. "I doubt I'd be able to break away, Ma'am. The conference begins that night as well."

"Well, come to tea if you can," Christina said. "We'd love to have you. Rutherford Grange is our home, just down the road from Westenra House. Do come, if you can."

"I'll try, Miss Christina," I said, but had my doubts. From what little I had seen of Sir Henry, it was unlikely he'd permit a mere peon like myself to leave during the conference for any reason, and besides, the more I thought of it, the more uncomfortable I felt. The Rutherfords were lovely and charming people, but far too gullible for my taste. As for Miss Gianetti—well, it pained me to see such an intelligent, beautiful woman waste her time indulging in confidence tricks. She could have been so much more.

"And we need to get going," Roxton put in. "You're exhausted, Althea; we should get you back home." He turned to me. "Goodbye, Mr. Dickson, it was a pleasure meeting you." We shook, and he shot me a glance that read: *I'll take care of everything. Let me handle this.*

"Goodbye, Lord John, Mrs. Rutherford. Goodbye, Miss Christina, Miss Gianetti." I watched as they all piled in the car and slowly drove away. I waved as the young women waved to me, and stood as the motor pulled out of the village and vanished into the countryside. I remained there musing for a moment, then looked around. Fortunately, the post office was right next to the station. I went inside and said, "I would like to send a telegram to Paris, please."

I knew a reporter there, a fellow about my own age. I sent this message:

Joseph:
I need a favor. See what you can find on a metaphysician calling himself Sâr Dubnotal. It's important.
Harry

I told the man to have it delivered to Westenra House as soon as an answer came back, and left. No, it was none of my business, but I had to admit that Mr. Blake had been proved right after all—a little background research never hurt anyone. My "extracurricular" activities complete, I went looking for the ride Sir Henry had promised me.

CHAPTER THREE

Westenra House was some three miles east of Wolfsbridge, so it would be a bit of a ride. Fortunately, the Sun was out, the air was fresh, and the scenery was most pleasant I have always loved the English countryside. It is, in part, one of the reasons I never returned to live in my home country. Yes, America has its places of beauty, great beauty; but I have always found something soothing about the ancient green fields of England, its hedges and wildflower-ringed walking paths. Traveling along them gives me a refreshing of the spirit very few other places can offer. I felt myself relaxing for the first time in two days and mused that perhaps serving as a mere security agent wouldn't be such a bad thing after all. Not if the weather kept up like this.

Of course, it would have helped if the driver of the small pony-driven trap I was seated upon enjoyed a decent conversation along with the scenery. Instead, I had a taciturn Scot whose main capacity for dialogue seemed to be the word "Urmmm."

"Lovely day, isn't it?"

"Urmmm."

"Is it very far to Westenra House?"

"Urmmm."

"Did you know I am secretly the Tsar of the Russians come to steal all your English women?"

"Urmmm."

A most scintillating conversationalist, he.

Resigning myself to a silent ride, I leaned back in the seat and resolved to simply enjoy the scenery. Here and there were fresh, grassy pastures dotted with sheep or cows, there, a farmer out in his fields plowing behind an old horse. Pleasant sights. As the cart rounded around a long corner in the road, to my right I glimpsed a small gravel driveway with an ancient gate leading into the fields; a faded wood sign entitling it. *Rutherford Grange* scrawled the dim letters.

"Ah," I said aloud without realizing it, "So that's where Miss Christina lives."

My statement seemed to shake my companion out of his dour silence for the first time. The old Scot turned his head, looked at me, and asked: "Aye? So ye've met the Rutherfords, then?"

"I had the pleasure, yes. At the station."

He blinked. "Aye? Did she howl, then?"

"Howl?" This was the second time I had heard that word used in conjunction with the Rutherfords. "No! Whatever do you mean by that?"

"Nothin', lad," the Scot replied, turning eyes back to the road. "Nothin' at all. Be comin' up on the House in a minute."

And indeed very shortly the cart reached the border of a long, high brick wall, stretching out alongside the road. We traveled beside this for several hundred yards until we reached an open, wrought-iron gate, and the driver guided the pony through it. We entered into a thick clump of trees, which quickly thinned out into a spacious, well-kept garden, and I received my first look at Westenra House.

It was, without doubt, the most pompously dull edifice I have ever seen.

Even after all these years I find it difficult to find the words to describe just how the appearance of Westenra House put me off. The problem did not lie anywhere in its actual physical structure: it was a large, three-story mansion of the most modern design with two extensive wings jutting off from the main hall. If anyone else had been living there it would have been quite attractive. But with the Westenras owning it... well.

Perhaps this will help me explain. I have been in many manor houses over the years, from the richly opulent to the genteelly decrepit. Yet from palatial to worn out, magnificent to falling to shambles, in each there was always an air of individuality, of actually being *lived in;* a sense of familiar comfort. Even with the most conceited, socially-climbing matron you can name, in a house filled with the most expensive furniture and priceless bric-a-brac you can think of, there was always a sense of a place where memories were made and kept precious, where hearts were found and broken and mended again. A sense of home.

Westenra House had none of that.

As said before, it was physically attractive enough, but it had no comfort. It was too cold, too austere. If the young Westenras had been raised there, there would have been no laughter in the halls, no toys on the floor. It was a building meant only to show how rich and important the owners were, how far above they were over all others, a museum to the Westenras' greatness and nothing more. A mausoleum trying to be the Coliseum.

I could tell my silent driver felt it, too, for a veiled look of disgust passed over his face as he gazed at the place. But he said nothing and guided the trap around to the back, then pointed me roughly to a small door. Obviously one of the servants' entrances. I certainly stood highly in Sir Henry's esteem.

"Knock loud," the driver advised me in a mutter. "Someone'll hear ye eventually. Prob'bly Colleen." He gave me a sidelong look. "Ye'll find she's a pretty lass," he added, a brief half-smile twisting his face. Then he was nicking the reins, and I barely had time to grab my bag and leap out before the trap started moving back toward the stables.

"Thank you!" I called, but the driver only replied back with an extra-loud "Urmm." I took that as an "You're welcome." Then I turned towards the door. No sense turning back now. I walked up and rapped the knocker loudly. There was no answer. I knocked again.

Hmmm, I thought, *a maid named Colleen.* Suggestive of an Irish lass, young, red-haired and pretty. I had already had the great fortune to meet two extraordinarily beautiful women today and it had put my youthful imagination in a mood for feminine company. Almost unconsciously I was already slicking my hair back, envisioning golden-red hair and eyes as emerald as the fabled Isle. I knocked once more, waiting for the gorgeous creature that would undoubtedly answer.

The door flew open, a cat dashed out and entangled itself between my legs. So surprised was I that I involuntarily stepped back, right on the creature's tail; it yowled and swiped my calf with an extended claw. Now I yowled, made an odd sort of jiggy dance with my feet, slipped on the cat again and fell right down. With an indignant "Mrrrowrr!" the cat dashed off and left me sitting upon my dignity.

A howl of merriment met me. I looked up, reproachfully, to see, not an Irish beauty, but a dark-skinned, square-jawed and unquestionably masculine figure leaning against the doorpost, laughing uproariously.

My greeter was a young East Indian youth about my own age, with quick, intelligent eyes shining with mirth at my predicament. I had to admit he was quite handsome. The unfortunate stereotype of the Indian is that of a wasted, stick-thin figure with ribs showing, dressed in a dirty loincloth and turban. But this man was tall and strapping, broad in shoulder and thick in arm. His rough hands and hard build showed many years of hard labor, but his dark, smooth skin was unblemished by weather, acne or disease. His head was bare, but a neat pointed beard bristled on the tip of his chin. Even his teeth were excellent, better than many Europeans I knew. An air of pride and confidence hung about him, and, if it were not for the uniform that marked him as some sort of servant, one might almost have taken him for the master of the house.

He laughed immoderately at me for quite a while. I could only sit and look at him. It, the laughter that is, seemed to be something he hadn't done in a long time "A—are you all right?" he finally managed to get out at last, between guffaws. "Did you hurt anything?"

"Only my pride," I grumbled, feeling my backside. Grinning, the young Indian reached down and helped me up.

"I'd advise you to stay out of Colleen's way from now on if I were you," he told me. "She has a long memory and doesn't take kindly to people who stumble over her."

"Colleen's the cat?"

"Of course. This is her favorite door. Open it once and, swoosh, she's gone. What were you expecting?" He read the look on my face and laughed again. "Ah, I see. Old Jack's been having one of his little jokes again. No, Colleen's just the kitchen cat—not some Irish lovely."

"Wonderful," I muttered, dusting myself off"

"Seriously, may I help you?"

49

"Harry Dickson. Here to help with security for the conference."

"Oh. So you're one of the detectives, eh?" The young Indian rolled his eyes. "Gods, that conference. For the past two months, Sir Henry's been on nothing but 'conference, conference, conference' and he blows up at the slightest delay. Everyone in the House will get on their knees and give thanks when that thing's over. I was under the impression it supposed to be some sort of secret, but by now everyone in the whole bloody county knows about it. Anyway, come in. Mr. Appleby's in the kitchen—he'll probably be the one to talk to."

I entered a long, narrow servant's corridor, white-washed and bare. It ran the entire width of the house, terminating at one end and turning a corner towards the rear That, I surmised, lead toward the kitchen. "This way," the youth said, and guided me in that direction.

As we strolled, I commented, "Would it be too much to ask whose hospitality it is I'm currently enjoying?"

"My apologies. My name is Kritchna. Darshan Kritchna."

"Harry Dickson," I said again, and we shook hands. "If I may ask, what do you do here?"

Kritchna paused for a moment, then said: "Whatever Sir Henry thinks is beneath the white servants."

"Ah. Well." There seemed to be nothing to add to that, so I changed the subject. "So, how long have you been with Sir Henry? Did you come with him from India?"

"*No!*" Kritchna burst out so suddenly and sharply it was nearly a shout. For a split-second his dark eyes flashed fire. But just as quickly it was gone. "I mean, no," he said, in a much quieter, calmer voice. "I... came over on a ship about a year and a half ago. Working my way over. I've only been at the House about six months now."

"I see." I frowned. The answer had been a simple enough one, but—perhaps it was merely my overactive detective instincts. Yet for some peculiar reason, I had the unaccountable feeling my companion was holding something back. Why should Kritchna have such a strong reaction to such a simple question? It wasn't anything unusual for officials to bring home particularly favored native servants from India.

I mused, but put the questions to the back of my mind. No use looking for mysteries when there were none. "You speak English very well," I said.

Kritchna nodded absently. "Self-taught, mostly. A little missionary schooling," he muttered, but distantly, as if thinking about something else. But by now we had entered the kitchen, and put any more conversation aside.

The kitchen was, to all appearances, the antithesis of the cold, too-showy exterior of the House. It was smaller than most from similar-sized homes, but was comfortable and warm, like a well-loved family dining area. Utensils and other kitchen paraphernalia hung in a cozily haphazard fashion everywhere—those with a beloved, absent-minded aunt or uncle will know what I mean—and the air was thick with the friendly, clean scents of soap, onions, linen and fresh-baked bread. A flour-haired old woman was bending over a huge pot of spicy-smelling soup. "Where's Mr. Appleby, Mrs. Mulligan?" Kritchna asked her.

The old woman looked up from her stirring and smiled kindly. "Out," she said with a thick Irish accent.

"Th' Master called for him. He should be back any moment. Who's this?"

"Fellow named Dickson. Here to help with the conference."

"Oh." She nodded pleasantly at me. "Nice t'meet you, Mr. Dickson. Darshan, Colleen didn't get out when you opened the door, did she?"

Kritchna shrugged, smiling. "Have you ever known her not to?"

"Oh, Darshan!" She tossed the spoon aside with a clatter. "Now I'll have t'go find her. You know how the Master hates to see her wanderin' around the yard. Here, you get over here and stir this soup. I'll be right back." Removing her apron, she toddled out of the kitchen. Unruffledly, Kritchna picked up the spoon and took her place. "Want some soup?" he asked casually.

I was about to decline but a growl from my stomach overruled me. "Yes, please. Thank you."

Kritchna poured a thick, steaming goulash of vegetables and meat into a bowl and shoved it over toward me. "Tea's in the kettle over there," he offered, and I was quick to help myself. The soup was excellent, and my stomach thanked me again and again.

But I also wished to know more about my curious companion. So I attempted to steer him into conversation again: "Are you the only Indian on the staff?" He nodded briefly, his attention on the soup. "Do you like working for Sir Henry?"

He looked up at me wryly. "Would you?" he demanded.

I had to admit he had me there. "No," I admitted.. "To be perfectly frank, I'm only here because my employer wishes it. But if he's that bad, why do you stay?"

"I have my reasons," Kritchna said gruffly. "And, 'to be perfectly frank,' they're not any of your business."

I was properly abashed. "You're right. I apologize. It was rude of me to inquire."

Kritchna sighed deeply and gave me a sheepish smile. "No. Forgive me. Sir Henry doesn't have a monopoly on boorish behavior. Seriously, working around here is fine—as long as you stick with the rest of the servants. They're all right. Mind you, Mr. Appleby can come on a bit strong at times—but you'll see that for yourself. Otherwise, he's quite a decent bloke—a bit too dignified, but fair." He sighed again. "But, as for the Westenras... they're... they're..." He paused, taking a deep breath as if searching for the words. Or trying to erase a bad memory. "I get along well enough with Peter," he said at last. "He's not a bad sort. Weak as anything, and, well, you know, being that he's—"

"What?"

Kritchna seemed to realize he has said too much. "Nothing."

"No, what? If I'm to work here I'd better know something about who I'm working for."

"Well..." Kritchna mused a moment. "All right," he said, "But if you ever tell anyone I told you this, I'll deny it. Understand?" I nodded. "All right. Peter Westenra is... well, he's—" The young servant sighed. "Well, perhaps you've heard he doesn't pay much attention to the women in the village?"

"Not exactly," I admitted, thinking of Christina Rutherford. "But I've heard of something along those lines."

"Ah. Well, let's just say…there are certain *reasons* for his lack of interest. Do you think you understand?"

"Oh," I replied, realizing.

Here was something not in the files, and little wonder. If Peter Westenra was what I was grasping, that revelation would mean scandal and social ruin to a man like Sir Henry. An ordinary family would not be able to live with such a reputation, let along an arrogant, grasping ass such as Sir Henry. The only counter would be to arrange some sort of a legitimate marriage as a cover—which explained that whole affair Christina Rutherford had mentioned earlier. To hide the embarrassment of his son, Sir Henry had obviously tried to force the boy to 'court' Christina. For whatever reason, it had fallen flat.

I had to admit I wondered why. From all reports, Peter was a smart man, certainly more intelligent than his sire. He would have known the dangers of *not* appearing absolutely normal in Society. If he found himself unable to curb his desires within the bonds of an ordinary, if unwanted marriage, there were ways around such vows. Men and women of "normal" appetites did so all the time. Surely he would have seen the benefits a marriage, even a fake one, would have given him careerwise and socially.

But Kritchna was continuing.

"Obviously, you might think that Sir Henry doesn't get on too well with his younger son. But he also can't just deny him because of the effects it'll have on his position. So they keep him quiet and under wraps, like a sheep." He smiled. "Ironically, everyone in town already knows. About Peter, I mean. But they keep it quiet...not for Sir Henry's sake, but for his. I know it's strange, but the fact is, everybody rather likes him. Far more than they do his father or brother. He's... well, he's *good*. Not at all like the rest of his family. They..."

The young Indian's voice trailed off. Then his jaw clamped smartly shut, as if he had definitely decided not to say something. " Peter'll be at the conference, but he'll be expected to do little but sit and nod and agree with whatever his father or brother says. I have to say I feel a bit sorry for him."

Silently I agreed. I could imagine it—a pale, sickly child, probably quite sensitive, born into a domineering family like the Westenras. And then discovering just why he preferred the company of boys. It must have made for many painful experiences as he was growing up.

Kritchna was looking away, seemingly lost in thought. Then he said: "Look, let's just forget the whole thing. Would you care for more soup?"

"Please," I replied, and about that time Mrs. Mulligan returned, carting a small black-and-white tabby: "There's my Colleen. There's my pretty lass." I swore the feline gave me the most miffed look. I made a mental note to keep away from her in future. Just in case.

We had just finished eating when the door opened and a pudgy, middle-aged man strode in. He was small and balding, with grey hair on the sides, but comported himself with the regality and dignity of all butlers (which ofttimes was far more than that which their masters possessed). He was holding a thick, black book beneath his arm that I recognized as *The Book of Common Prayer*. "Ah, Darshan, there you are," he said. "I need to speak with you. It just so happens that late yesterday afternoon, I—oh, hello, young man. And whom might you be?"

I stood. "Harry Dickson, here for the conference."

"Ah, yes, one of the security men. A moment, young man, and I'll escort you to the library. Sir Henry will give you your instructions from there. Now, then,

Mr. Kritchna—early last night I called you and couldn't find you for about an hour. Where were you?"

"Oh," Kritchna squirmed in his chair, "I was doing something for Sir Henry, Mr. Appleby."

Appleby drew himself up. "I doubt that, for I asked the Master if he had called for you, and he said no. Now, really—where were you? And don't tell me you were out helping at the stables. I checked there, as well."

"All right, all right." Kritchna threw up his hands. "I confess. I snuck into town for an hour and went to the cinema."

"Darshan!"

"It was a *Little Neddy* picture!"

Appleby groaned and put his hand to his forehead. "Darshan, Darshan, what am I going to do with you? Sneaking off from your duties! And you know how I feel about cinemas! If the Master found out, you would be dismissed at once."

"Well, if it's any consolation, the picture wasn't that good."

The butler sighed. "It most certainly is not. But I shall deal with you later. Come along, young man, and I'll take you to the library. But you remain right where you are, Mr. Kritchna—we have a few matters to discuss."

With a sympathetic glance at Kritchna, I rose from the table. Appleby escorted me out from the servants' quarters into the House proper.

Now I knew why the kitchen had seemed so homey and comfortable in stark contrast to the cold and ostentatious outside of the House—obviously none of the Westenras ever choose to set foot there. It would be beneath them to enter any room where mere servants dwelt. But out here, where the masters of the house lived, things were different. Everything had been carefully and selectively chosen for the glory of Sir Henry Westenra.

There was not a room I passed that did not have at least one portrait of Sir Henry, or Alexander, looming in majestic bombastity over the rich carpet and mahogany walls. Sneering down upon the peons with stiff-upper-lip superiority. No expense had been spared to give that impression. The furnishings themselves were, naturally, of the most elegant and expensive sort—very beautiful, but bought to show off Sir Henry's wealth and taste rather than to be actually *used*. The whole interior of Westenra House, outside the kitchen, reeked of the same dead, loveless elegance its exterior did. I

I could not imagine the conference being a success in a place like this. Everyone would be too afraid they'd track mud upon the carpets.

"The library," Appleby's said, and opened the door for me.

It was much as I had expected. Filled wall-to-wall with rare and expensive books, not one of which had ever been cracked open. I hated to see such a thing. A library should smell pleasantly of wood pulp, with the pages of each volume yellowing and well-thumbed, used and loved. Not treated as some sort of untouchable museum piece.

Did I say that the books were all uncracked? I stand corrected—for as I watched Appleby crossed the room to a small, obscure shelf where there was a gap between volumes. Carefully and reverently, he replaced his copy of *The Book of Common Prayer*.

"Your employer allows you to use the library?" I asked, rather astounded.

The butler harrumphed at the unexpected question, coughed, turned slightly red. "This small shelf is permitted for the servants' use, young man. I keep my own books here. If I'm not overstepping my bounds, sir, may I ask—are you a believer?"

"Hm?" I looked at him in puzzlement. Thinking back to my train ride, I inwardly groaned. God, not another Spiritualist, please! "A believer in what?"

The butler held up his book—which I now saw was the Bible. "A believer in the Word, sir; in the Holy Bible and the death and resurrection of Our Lord, the Holy Son of God."

I breathed a sigh of relief. "Oh, that! Thank goodness—I thought you were going to say Spiritualism."

"Spiritualism? Oh, heavens, no, no, no. Total rubbish, and Satanic rubbish at that! I'll have none of that!"

I smiled. "Well, then, we have something we can agree on—at least in regards to Spiritualism being "rubbish. I don't believe in the Devil, though. I'm not a Christian."

"I see, sir."

"Does that offend you?"

"No, sir; that's your concern. But I must admit it disappoints me to find so few Christians these days. The Spiritualist obsession in this country..." he shook his head. "The Bible explains the existence of life after death perfectly well! Where is people's faith?"

I shrugged "Faith is fine, until you actually reach a point where all you've heard about faces you. Then you want facts. You want to know your loved one is all right; you don't want pats on the head and comforting murmurings of 'have faith.' Ergo, the popularity of Spiritualism Why do you need faith when you can simply 'talk' to your loved one and find out the truth?"

"I suppose," the butler said. "But I still think it's evil. The Enemy will use all at his disposal to lure men from the Truth. Spiritualism is just another tool in his arsenal."

"Perhaps," I said, not wanting to get into it. I thought of Sir John. "Then again, perhaps if it makes some people happy, then there's a reason for it."

"You're speaking of the Rutherford séance?"

"Yes. How did you know?"

"It's common knowledge, I'm afraid. I must admit, it truly upsets me to see Mrs. Rutherford so wounded. She and her daughter are fine Christian people. Even if Miss Rutherford, if you'll excuse me for saying so, can be a bit too exuberant at times. But their faith should have been strong enough to see them through this. I'm sorry to see that it is not." He paused before a door. "But enough of that. Gossiping is a sin, and one I must overcome. Please pardon me. If you'll wait in here, I'll fetch Sir Henry."

"Thank you," I said and the butler left, leaving me alone with books never read. I glanced around, looking at the titles. As I suspected, no real attempt at ordering had been done; they were simply shoved inside according to size and color of cover. Here was a first edition of *Pickwick Papers*, there a history of South America, there a old, rare of volume of Arronax's sea life encyclopedias, there *Hamlet*. I found myself reaching up and plucking the books off the shelf at random. If the Westenras would not use their own library, I thought, I would. Glancing up, I saw a large, black, folio-sized volume. There was no title upon the spine. Idly I reached for it, then paused. There was something within the volume I had honestly not expected to see.

A bookmark.

A simple paper bookmark, tucked low down among the pages so you would not have noticed it unless you were right before the volume. Curious, I carefully opened the cover to the title page to read:

JOURNAL OF CHRISTOPHER WESTENRA
(1663-1664)

A journal! I never would have thought a Westenra would have kept one. Then again, I would never have thought a Westenra having the intelligence to be able to write. But I was being cruel. Gently fingering the book-mark, I flicked it open to the pages it marked, some-where in the middle of the book. It read:

"I have buried the body under the bridge where no one will think to look for it. As soon as we have a good flood, the grave will be smoothed out. I dare not let any-one know what I have discovered. If it should be learned, I would be the one hanging off the edge of the bridge, not the Rutherf—"

Voices behind me caused me to slam the book shut and quickly replace it back on the shelf. The door opened and Appleby came in, followed by a very red-faced, very indignant Sir Henry.

"Sir Henry, this is Mr. Dick—" the butler began but Westenra cut him off.

"So, you finally decided to come, eh?" he snorted, glaring at me. "I'm surprised you even had sense to get on the right train. Very well, now that you're here, you may as well be useful. The rest of the security staff won't be arriving until tomorrow, so there's nothing for you to do—so go out to the stables and see if you can lend a hand out there. They always need someone to clean up after the horses. Not what you signed up for,

I'm sure, but I never waste men or time. I won't have any layabouts here. Later, you can get the feel of the place. But whatever you don't, don't mess up! This conference is too damned important. I spent months trying to get the wretched French over here, and I won't have anything spoil it now! Damn them anyway, miserable Frogs and their concerns about what we're doing to the natives in India. They're our wogs, not theirs. We'll do what we like with them. Frogs and Wogs, what a combination, eh?" He glowered at me, as if expecting me to answer. I could swear his mustache actually flapped.

I wouldn't give him the satisfaction of answering. Appleby just looked embarrassed. Instead, I said: "Whatever you like, Sir Henry. And may I ask about my sleeping quarters?"

"Oh," Westenra shrugged dismissively. "Yes. Well, space is at a premium here with the conference, so most of the arrivals' aides will be rooming with the servants. I planned to have the security staff sleep out in the stables with the men out there. Since you're here, I guess we can put you up with our house Indian, what's his name, Appleby?"

"Kritchna sir, Darshan Kri—"

"Yes, Kratchna. You can sleep with him tonight. Ordinarily, I wouldn't think of putting any white man with a wog, but you have to make do when you have to. What do you think of that, Mr. Dickson?" He looked at me smugly.

"That would be excellent." I replied coolly. "I've already had the opportunity to meet Mr. Kritchna and would be glad to have him as a roommate."

Sir Henry looked at me bemusedly. Clearly he had been expecting another answer. Then he shrugged: "Suit yourself. Appleby, show Mr. Dickson to the stables for now. I'm sure they can find something useful for him to do." He turned to leave.

"Oh, Sir Henry," I called, "one more thing."

"What?"

"I look forward to meeting your son Peter. Is he here?"

"Peter?" Sir Henry wheeled about. "Why would anyone want to meet him? Yes, yes, he'll be here, if he's not too drunk to walk. But I wouldn't get too friendly with him." He gave a wicked smirk. "He might take it the wrong way." He turned on his heel and stalked out.

I glanced over at Appleby. Once he had been certain his master was no longer in sight, he had leaned against the wall and gave a groan. "Sir, I apologize... it's just Sir Henry's way..."

"Never mind, Mr. Appleby," I said. "Just take me to the stables After the air in here, horse dung would smell far sweeter."

After a rather filthy rest of the afternoon, I ate dinner with the rest of the staff in the kitchen. I sat next to Kritchna, and Appleby led the table with great dignity and good manners. To his credit, he forced neither of us to join him and the rest in prayer before and after the meal. Afterwards, most of the staff left for bed or their other duties, while Appleby sat reading his Bible, waiting for any call. Tomorrow, I would learn my exact duties and master the grounds of the House, and so wished to retire early. Kritchna had no other duties, so we both said goodnight and trooped upstairs.

Kritchna's room was at the very top of the House, just off the attic. At the door, he paused. "Welcome to the Wolfsbridge Savoy," he said, "Please, make yourself comfortable." And he opened to the smallest, most wretched garret I had ever been inside.

It was barely bigger than a closet. There were no furnishings for there was no room for them, just a small, rickety bed with a pillow shoved inside. There was barely enough room for one man to walk beside it. One lone window, a porthole really, let in what light there was. And there was precious little of that even in the daytime, for the roof above slanted down, neatly blocking the majority of the view. There weren't even actual walls, for the builders had simply left the bare wooden skeleton of the timbers showing. Kritchna slipped in, bent under the bed and pulled out a candle. With a match from his pocket, he lit it and then grandly gestured me inside. "The Royal Suite."

"Good Lord, this is ridiculous," I exclaimed. "In a house this large, the other servants should get regular rooms, even the tweenies. Why do you get this?"

In reply Kritchna simply ran his hand down the brown pallor of his skin. I bit off an obscenity.

"I'm used to it by now," Kritchna said, starting to pull off his clothes. "Just something else my people have to put up with."

"Oh, for—but, look, Kritchna... Darshan. I don't know you very well, but you're obviously an intelligent, gifted man. Why are you in Service? Surely there's something else better you can be doing rather than this. Working for the Foreign Office as a translator, perhaps, or..."

"As I said, I have my reasons for being here," Kritchna answered, just a little too sharply for me not to take note. "Now, move over, I've got to put this blanket out in the hall."

"Whyever for?"

"Where do you think I'm going to sleep? You get the bed."

"You mean Sir Henry expects you to give up your own bed for me?"

"For a white man, yes."

"Nonsense." I was appalled. "I'm not about to kick you out of your bed just so I can have one. I'll sleep in the hall."

"No, you shan't. If Sir Henry catches you, he'll have both our heads. He may not like you, but you're still white. He expects you to behave as one."

"I'd be ashamed to call myself a white man if I kicked another man out of bed just so I could have it. Look. There's just enough room for the two of us. Why don't we share?"

Kritchna looked skeptical. "Share the bed?"

"Why not? At least that way we both get a bit of mattress."

"If you can call this piece of petrified timber a mattress. I've slept on iron bunks that were softer. But—all right. But you get the side by the wall. If someone comes up here, I have to hit the floor fast."

"Fine," I replied, and quickly changed to my own nightshirt. I crawled in next to Kritchna (the mattress groaning as I did) and he blew out the candle.

"Just like Ishmael and Queequeg, eh?" Kritchna chuckled.

"You've read that?"

"Oh, yes. My grandfather was well-versed in literature, both Eastern and Western. I've read lots of things. Just remember to keep your great white whale to yourself, sahib."

"Ha. No problem there." We turned our backs to each other and closed our eyes.

I couldn't sleep. Which was unusual: for most my life I've been able to sleep anywhere, unfamiliar surroundings or no. Irritably I drew the lone blanket up closer. I felt cold. But no matter how tight I pulled, not matter how I curled up my body to conserve heat, I could not get warm. And this on a summer night that would ordinarily make me perspire. Further, I was starting at every sound: the gentle whisper of bat wings over the roof, the creaking of settling floorboards, the hoot of an owl. Finally, I jerked up as the sound of tiny, regular pattering sounded on the tiles above us. *Pat-pat-pat-pat-pat-pat.* It traveled quickly down the slope of the roof, then up, then back down again. A rat? I wondered. Then I heard a piping little mew.

"It's Colleen," Kritchna murmured sleepily next to me. "She climbs upon the roof at nights. You get used to it."

"Mmm," I mumbled, slipping back down. Mentally I admonished myself. It must have been all the talk of Spiritualism earlier, I thought. Playing games with my subconscious, making me jump at every little sound as if afraid a Spirit might jump out and seize me. Foolish. You know better than that, Dickson.

Above, Colleen continued with her contented mewling. *Enjoy yourself, my girl*, I thought and started drifting to sleep again.

That was when I heard the other noise.

I say without exaggeration that it was the strangest sound I have ever heard. Heavy, and regular, spaced precisely like footsteps. *Thump. Thump. Thump.* But there was something odd, something wrong about each noise. Something incomplete I should say, as if whatever was causing it was something very big and very heavy and yet—somehow not fully solid. Like something only partly filled, something not quite fully *complete*. The best way I can describe it is as if someone had a great rubber bag half-filled with water and was steadily dropping it upon the roof, so its echo sounded more like *"Schtwhump."* And it was continuing—*Schtwhump, schtwhump, schtwhump....*

"What the hell is that?" Kritchna grunted, rising up in the bed.

"Dunno," I replied. "Could someone have gotten on the roof?"

Whatever it was, it was moving steadily, if wetly, down toward the edge. Directly above us, Colleen the cat was still meowing, but suddenly fell silent just as the *schtwhump*ing stopped. We could hear her hiss violently. Then there was a great, frightened "MRRROOWWWWWW!!!" and suddenly the little porthole that served as our window shattered into pieces! Kritchna and I both clambered up clumsily, knocking into each other and trying to avoid falling glass, as we stumbled to the edge of the bed and over.

"Damnation!" roared Kritchna. "What the bloody hell is going on? Where's that damn candle?" There was the scratch of a match and the tiny pinprick of flame shone dimly. Kritchna raised the candle up. "What happened?"

"Something came through the window," I snapped obviously, climbing back upon the bed. My hands pressed against several pieces of glass, cutting myself, but I ignored it. "But God knows—oh my!" I drew back. Kritchna leaned forward, holding the candle out. He swallowed.

There on the bed, lying in a bloody heap, was the tiny, twisted body of Colleen.

Her head had been completely severed from her neck.

CHAPTER FOUR

Shards of falling glass had rained on our hair, skin and clothing, or bit painfully into our feet as we stepped blindly about in the darkness. But our discomfort was as nothing compared to the still, small form lying grotesquely upon the pillow before us; a small, intensely crimson geyser of lifeblood pouring out of the maw of her neck.

Where her head might be, neither of us could say.

"Hell," I heard Kritchna mutter blackly, unable to tear his eyes from the horrible sight. "Is that Colleen? What could have done this? An owl?"

I refrained from replying. I was too busy snatching the candle from my reluctant roommate, leaning forward for a closer examination of the body. It was true owls often preyed upon cats. My mentor had made a point once of showing me how various animals killed, and owls had been among them. The one I had witnessed had struck the back of the creature's neck with its beak, instantly snapping it, but did not shear the head clear off. For a moment, I debated whether a shard of glass might have severed through the cat's neck, but no; I would've expected the wound to be more jagged. This was very neat and even. I felt a wave of disgust as I ran my fingers through the bloody fur, trying to peer through the gusher of life, but after a moment, I found tiny marks about what remained of the neck, bearing no sign of having been made by beak or glass. They were deep and even, and could possibly have been made by talons, but somehow I found myself doubting it. In fact, if I didn't know any better, I could swear these were...

…teeth marks.

Scthwump, schtwump wump wump wump—

Kritchna and I shot looks at each other. There it was again—the wet, sucking, peculiarly incomplete sound we had heard just before the cat had come crashing down upon our heads. It pattered with its strange sloshing swiftly along the edge of the eave outside—and then, what small sliver of the moon Kritchna's tiny window let in was suddenly darkened and we heard a great whuffing sound and the snapping of branches. Whatever it was had either leaped or fallen out off the roof, down to the bushes some three stories below!

Hastily, I scrambled to my feet on top of the bed, ignoring the glass and slippery pools of blood soaking into the mattress. If I could just get my head out the window—no good. Not all the pane had shattered, but what remained had turned into transparent jagged knives of glass: I'd behead myself like Colleen if I dared try stick my head out the opening. I fumbled with the lock but was again frustrated. Disuse had rusted the hatch. Below I could hear something struggling in the foliage. Leaping to the floor (and nearly knocking Kritchna over in the process), I yelled: "Come on!" and threw open the door. If we hurried, we might just make it in time—

—To slam right into Mr. Appleby.

"Great God Almighty!" the butler exclaimed—and for such a devout Christian to say something like that meant he was very annoyed indeed. "What is the meaning of this ruckus? Do you wish to wake the masters? Explain yourselves at once!"

"See for yourself," I snapped back, jerking my thumb back toward the bed. Obviously I was being rude, but time was of the essence. I pushed past the butler, dashed down the small flight of stairs, through the hall, down the main stairway and out the huge front door to find—

—Nothing, save for the chirruping of insects and the occasional call of night birds. The gardens surrounding the House were silent. Nothing stirred, nothing appeared. The full Moon beamed down benevolently, bathing trees and bushes in an ethereal halo. You'd never imagine something slinking about it had just slaughtered an animal.

But the shrubs I wanted were along the west side of the House, and whatever it was might not have been able to have extricated itself yet. Still clad in nightshirt and bare feet, the dew cold on my still-bleeding soles, I made my way along the length of the House as swiftly and silently as possible, my ears pricked to catch the slightest disturbance. The window to Kritchna's garret would be right around this corner. I paused to listen; I could hear no rustling; no *schtwhumping*, nothing unusual to speak of. Taking a deep breath, I whipped around the corner, prepared for anything, to find—

—Nothing again. Absolutely nothing. Just a clump of flattened rosebushes, the stems bent and broken as if a great weight had crashed upon them. My prey, whatever it had been, had escaped.

I scanned the ground for footprints, indentations, anything that might tell me the direction my fugitive went. But even in the soft, dewy grass, I found no sign of anything. Yet something was shining on the flowers in the moonlight, something thick and sparkling, like dew only much more viscous.

"Find anything?"

I nearly jumped as I found Kritchna waiting beside me. So intent had I been on my examination, I hadn't even heard him approach. I also noted he had had the presence of mind to pull on a pair of pants and shoes before joining me. As well as having brought an electric torch. I felt rather like kicking myself.

"Appleby's upstairs trying to find a hatbox or something for Colleen," he said. "Discovered anything?"

"Nothing yet," I admitted reluctantly. "But, here, shine that torch here a moment. I want to see something."

Kritchna complied. As the beam flashed over the broken flowers, his face screwed up in distaste. "What on Earth is that mess?"

That mess was a concoction the like of which I had never seen in any chemistry laboratory; a clear, sticky, pus-like substance dribbling slowly down the stalks and petals like slow, cold treacle. The bushes were saturated with it, like those I tossed my water-filled paper bags upon out the windows of my brownstone as a boy in New York. It pooled slowly at the base of the plants, steadily soaking down into the ground. Wait—no, it wasn't! It was drawing into itself, shriveling into smaller blobs, evaporating into the air.

"What is it?" Kritchna asked.

"I'm not certain." I knelt to carefully swab a bit up, rubbing it between my fingers. Cool to the touch. Odorless, as well. I found myself wishing I had brought a specimen jar. The goop clung to the crushed branches and petals of the rosebushes. Peculiarly, I could find no trace of the same substance on the grass.

"Funny, though," Kritchna was continuing absently, having also taken up a bit to examine. "I could almost swear I have seen something like this before. If only I could remember where..."

With a sigh, I stood and wiped my hand on my shirt. "Well, whatever it is, it evaporates quickly. See?

It's almost all gone already. Who knows what it is, but it's clear we're not going to learn anything else about it tonight. We might as well go back inside."

We must have made a sorry sight as we tramped back upstairs, half-dressed, disheveled, and scratched in several places on our arms and legs. Appleby failed to be impressed. "Darshan, your blankets and sheets are simply soaked with blood. They're completely ruined!"

"Better them than us, Mr. Appleby," Kritchna stated wryly.

"Well…yes," the butler sighed, looking down at the bed. Resting on what remained of the mattress was a plain brown hatbox, lid closed. It didn't take a detective to guess what was inside. "Mrs. Mulligan shall not be pleased. Did you find out what it was?" I shook my head. "Well, perhaps it was an owl, then."

Somehow I sincerely doubted that, but as I had no better theory, I did not contradict him. Gently he made a little "cross" over the box with his fingers, and then picked it up.

"Well, I'd best get this somewhere for the night." He ran his gaze over us. "And find you some iodine and bandages. You've probably been bleeding all over the carpets, like as not. Heaven knows where I'm going to put you two; but you obviously can't sleep here tonight. You might as well take my room. I'll sleep on a divan in the hall."

Pleased and more than a little surprised at this generosity, we thanked him gratefully. He coughed. "Yes— well. I'd best be getting that iodine. Wait here." He quickly darted downstairs.

Kritchna turned to me and smiled. 'Told you he was all right. Just comes on a bit strong sometimes."

"You were right."

We moved to sit side-by-side on the steps, shaking the glass from our clothing. "Do you think it was an owl?" Kritchna asked at last, shuffling over to give me more room.

I shook my head. "I can't think of what else it could have been. Although I've never seen an owl do anything like that before. The only other creature it could be is a dog or a fox, and neither of those could've gotten up to the roof. Could they?"

Now it was Kritchna's turn to shake. "No. Colleen could climb just about anywhere she wanted, but nothing else. Still, that had to be the most disgusting thing I've ever seen."

I smiled, wryly. "Says the man who watches *Little Neddy* pictures."

"Hm?" Kritchna glanced at me puzzled. "What are you talking about? I hate *Little Neddy*."

I blinked at the confession. Had I or had I not very definitely heard him tell Appleby he had slipped away from his duties to see a motion picture in Wolfsbridge, only now to hear him say he couldn't stand the very star of the same?

The question must have been plainly visible on my face, for no sooner had it crossed my mind than Kritchna quickly changed the subject:

"So. How did you get into detective work? Did you always want to be one?"

The sudden change in topic did nothing to ease my suspicions, but I decided to go along with it for the nonce. "Pretty much. I've always admired great American detectives like Nick Carter and King Brady, and my father knew this old actor who used to be a Secret Service agent. He'd tell me and my sister all these old stories about his partner and himself in the Western states.

I'm certain he made half of them up, but I didn't care. And so, one day, I simply decided to make my living as a detective. Runs in the blood, I suppose. My father once tackled a few cases himself, with a master thief as a partner, of all things, and my sister even married a very influential private inquiry agent back in the States. Had a son. Little Franklin should be—oh, going on two or so by now. I've asked them to name the next after me, but for some reason my sister is dedicated to calling it 'Joseph' if it's a boy."

"Anyway, when Father sent me here for my education, I made a point of seeking other detectives out. Shortly after, I met my mentor, and the rest, as the cliché goes, is history. And you? Your family?"

"Ah." Kritchna shifted uneasily in his seat and for a moment it looked as if he'd almost rather talk about *Little Neddy*. "Well, my family's a bit difficult to talk about."

"Oh?" My eyebrow arched. "I only know a little of Indian society, but it's not a caste problem, is it? You're not an Untouchable or anything like that?"

"No!" Kritchna shook his head violently. "No. No, no, no. Nothing like that. We're Brahmins."

"Brahmins?" My astonishment only grew. "Then why on Earth are you in..."

"Service? For my own reasons, Dickson. But, back to my family—as I said, it's a bit difficult to explain them. We're not just of the Brahmin caste, you see—at least, so my family claims. What we are, what we've always traditionally been, is—well, I guess you would have to call us wizards."

I raised my eyebrows. "Wizards?"

"You know—Indian wizards. Fakirs and yogis and all that rot. We're supposed to come from a long line of them; Protectors of the Ancient Secrets and so on. It's all rubbish, of course. What we are is a bunch of street magicians—you can find thousands of them in any Indian city. Snake charmers, fire-walkers, things like that. We're just higher-caste than most."

I nodded, smiling, beginning to understand. "Yes, I know. My father's a magician; he taught me half those tricks himself."

"I'm sure. But to listen to my family, it was all real, at least once. We've just fallen on hard times, according to them. Once, we were supposed to be court magicians to Chandragupta himself, or so the stories go. The power's still in our blood, my great-uncle Nadir used to say—it's just waiting to be rediscovered. But my father was having none of it. He'd seen the signs—the English ruled India now, and it was their ways, not ours, that was going to shape the future. So he turned his back on it. My great-uncle was none too happy about his decision, for he wanted my sister and me to be his apprentices, but Father refused and that was that. My uncle's in the Philippines now, trying to re-find the magic, or so I've heard."

"You have a sister, then?"

"Had. She's gone now." The young Indian fell silent. Part of me wanted to ask more, but Kritchna's face had gone cold and stony. So I decided to refrain. Besides, Appleby was just coming back up with the iodine. Neither of us felt like playing Ishmael and Queequeeg now, so after retiring to Appleby's room, I slumped into a chair while Kritchna collapsed into the bed. As I was just about to drop off, I heard Kritchna murmur something softly that should have shot me straight up if I wasn't so exhausted. I forgot about it almost immediately.

"Y'know, I do remember where I've seen that stuff before. My great-uncle showed me some once."

"Really?" I yawned, not able to stay awake a moment longer. "What was it?"

"Oh, just something he said was used in his work. Ectoplasm, I think he called it."

Mrs. Mulligan was indeed not pleased upon learning the fate of her beloved Colleen the next morning, and spent most of breakfast sobbing inconsolably.

Mr. Appleby tried to comfort her as best he could, but to little avail. As for Kritchna and myself, we blinked, and yawned, and looked guiltily into our eggs, but said nothing. Things only became worse when Appleby admitted they would probably have to toss Colleen into the incinerator. With so much going on, the loss of a kitchen cat was low on the list of priorities.

Still, my duty was to assist with the conference, not deal with dead pets. So I dismissed Colleen and turned my mind to the matter at hand. The rest of the security should be arriving that afternoon, and Sir Henry would no doubt have a completely incompetent plan about what to do and when. I'd have to see what I could rearrange without his knowledge. And then there was—

I almost didn't notice Old Jack slipping a paper next to my plate. "This just came for ye," he said in the longest sentence I had heard from him yet and turned away. I tore it open. It was the response to the telegram I had sent to Joseph, answering the query I had about Miss Annunciata's mysterious employer the Sâr Dubnotal. It was short and sweet and simply read:

Harry:
Trust him.
Joseph.

I gazed bemusedly at the words. Trust him? Trust an obvious fraud, a man who preyed on the lonely and gullible, who espoused occult nonsense for a quick *sou*? I wondered what was wrong with Joseph. He was usually much more reliable.

"What's that, Dickson?"

"Oh," I crumpled the telegram in my hand. "Nothing, Kritchna. Just an answer to a query I had about the Rutherfords. I had the pleasure of meeting them yesterday."

"The Rutherfords," Mrs. Mulligan paused from her tears long enough to sigh. "Poor people. They're such dears. It's a shame, all the tragedy in their life."

"That reminds me. There's something Old Jack said to me yesterday I didn't understand. I mentioned Miss Christina and he asked 'Did she howl?' What on earth did he mean?"

Mrs. Mulligan and Appleby exchanged glances. "I'll speak with him," the butler rumbled and rose from the table. Mrs. Mulligan rubbed her forehead and sighed again.

I paused, waiting.

"Oh, dear, Mr. Dickson...we're really not supposed t' discuss it. The Rutherfords are fine Christian people—now. It's just that... well... once they weren't."

"Eh?"

"Old stories, Dickson," Kritchna put in. "Nobody really believes them anymore."

"No, do go on."

"Well.." Mrs. Mulligan looked around, seeming like she very much didn't want to be there. "You have t' unnerstand that, in the old days, the Rutherfords were just as important around here as the Master's family. They weren't as rich as the Westenras, but old family, you know? In fact, this area used to be called Rutherford's Green. But that got changed about the 17th century or so."

"How?"

Kritchna took pity on the woman. "I'll tell him, Mrs. Mulligan. Apparently back in the old days the Rutherfords were considered, shall we say, a bit too friendly with those sorts 'decent' people like the Westenras didn't associate with back then. You know, like Jews. And Catholics. And Gypsies. Especially Gypsies.

"Anyway, the story goes there was a small clan of them that would come around and camp out on the Rutherfords' land every few years, and old Roger Rutherford would go out and spend time with them. So much time rumor got around that he was learning things from them."

"Things such as?"

"Such as black magic, that's what."

I couldn't help but groan. A supernatural story, *again?* My mentor would have been having a conniption right about now.

Kritchna grinned at the expression upon my face. "Yes, I know, but there it is. It started getting round that Roger Rutherford was running around naked at night with the gypsies, engaging in all sorts of evil rites and things. For a while, Rutherford managed to block anything happening to him. But then the sheep started getting killed."

"Really."

"Oh, yes." He was warming to his story now. "The farmers stated some great hairy dog was traveling from farm to farm, slaughtering their animals. But no one ever got a good look at it until one night when one actually came right across the thing. It was big. Bigger than any dog had the right to be, the story goes. And it looked right at that farmer. And there, eyes glowing blood- red in the torchlight, it laughed at him."

"Like 'ha, ha,' yes. It stood there and it laughed at him, and then it ran away. No one had ever seen anything like it. So Christopher Westenra, he was the one who owned the House then, got a bunch of men together to go and hunt the thing. One night, they finally found it, and shot at it—but it got away. But not before Mr. Westenra had wounded it in the leg. And the story goes, they followed it, they followed the trail of blood it left, through the woods and over the fields—until it led right to Rutherford Grange. And inside, they found Roger Rutherford, with his wife and the Gypsy chief, with a wound to the leg

"I suppose you can guess what happened after that. Real dogs don't laugh at people, and how could they shoot it in the leg and find a man right after with a wound in the same leg? Roger Rutherford claimed that he had been out looking for the beast, too; that it was something brought by the Gypsies that had gotten away. He said it had attacked him and bit him in the leg. Nobody believed him. They accused him of being a werewolf; that the Gypsies had taught him how to change his shape, and dragged him and his wife and the old Gypsy chief out of the building and down to the town. They hauled them right to the bridge and without a trial or anything, they…"

"Hung them," I finished for him.. "Hence the name Wolfsbridge"

"Yes," Kritchna nodded, "And the killings stopped right after that, of course."

"Oh, for—"

"But the story doesn't stop here, sir," Mrs. Mulligan suddenly put in. "They say that Roger Rutherford swore one day he'd be back for revenge; that his ghost would return and haunt those responsible."

"*Every* ghost story has the victim saying *that*, Mrs. Mulligan. But I suppose they say ever since then on moonlit nights you can see a great dog bounding across the fields, laughing at everyone he meets."

"Actually, no, sir. Nothing like that's ever happened. And it got to be a joke around town that whenever you said something about a Rutherford, you had to say 'And did he howl?' I think it's awful. Anyway, after that, the Rutherfords—Roger's son was away at school—kind of fell on bad times. But they're good people, now. I hate to think that story's still following them after all these years."

I nodded. Something had come to my mind. "Would you excuse me?" I quickly left the table.

In a moment, I found myself back in the library. Glancing quickly about to see if anyone was present, I swiftly ran my eyes along the shelf, searching for the volume I had snuck a look at the afternoon before. Ah, there it was. Yes: *The Journal of Christopher Westenra*. Flipping quickly through the pages, I located the paragraph I had left off and hurriedly scanned the rest. This is what I read:

"*I have buried the body under the bridge where no one will think to look for it. As soon as we have a good flood, the grave will be smoothed out. I dare not let any-one know what I have discovered. If it should be learned, I would be the one hanging off the edge of the bridge, not the Rutherfords. Damn them and their wretched Gypsies! If they had just remembered their place, this never would have happened. Not that I'm sorry Ruther-ford is dead, but I will forevermore be looking over my shoulder. And damn the beast for not dying when first I shot it. It probably did attack Rutherford, just like he said. But the chance was too good to pass up. Now I am rid of an enemy. But the cost!*

"Still, at least the beast is truly dead now. I blew its head apart myself. I still have no idea what it is—it cer-tainly is neither dog nor wolf—but I am well rid of it. But if anyone should learn the truth, my life would be forfeit. May that never be. As for Rutherford's curse be-fore he went over; well—I should be king if I had a pen-ny for the times anyone has damned me. Still, the look on his face—but no. Once again my fears run away with me—"

"Reading something interesting?" came a mild voice.

I whipped around, terrified I was going to find Sir Henry or Alexander about to pounce upon me for read-ing their private histories. But instead, it proved to be a slight, fair-haired, sallow figure, good-looking in a weak way, who smiled gently at me and said, "Don't worry. I won't tell." He stuck out his hand. "You're the detective, aren't you? Harry Dickson? I'm Peter Westenra."

So this was the son I had not yet met, but had heard so much about. Peter Westenra. He looked awful. His eyes were red and bleary and his breath hissed with the stench of stale beer. Quite obviously young Westenra had been on the town the night before and was yet to recover. I confess, seeing what I had recently learned of his preferences, that I was leery of grasping the hand he held out. But he was, after all, my client, at least partly, and I took it. The grip was surprisingly firm, and he smiled self-depreciatingly as he said:

"I know it doesn't look it, but I really do hate gin. It's just that when it calls, I must answer." He laughed shortly. "I was just going along to the kitchen to get a glass of tomato juice. Care to come along?"

I must have mumbled something affirmative, trying to turn his attention from the fact I had just violated his family's privacy, but he seemed to take no offense at it. He kept up a patter of small talk as we returned to the kitchen. He nodded to Kritchna, who was still sitting there, then turned to the cook and said:

"Ah, Mrs. Mulligan. I heard what happened last night about poor Colleen. If I may ask, what were you planning on doing with—? What, the incinerator? No, no, no; that won't do; won't do at all. Look, there's a little corner of my garden that's rather secluded, why don't you bury her there? What Father doesn't know... no, no, that's all right, Mrs. Mulligan. I had a dog once as a boy, myself."

With his glass of tomato juice, he sat across from Kritchna and I. "So, Dickson, what do you think of Westenra House so far?

I paused. "Well," I began, "its architecture is certainly *unique—*"

"Oh, please. It's the bloody ugliest house in this part of the county," Peter smiled. "Not that I'd ever tell Father that, of course."

Despite myself, I found myself smiling back. Perhaps oddly, I found myself liking Peter Westenra. In addition, I was aware that Kritchna next to me seemed to relax more. Whatever else the young Indian may have thought of the rest of his employers, he didn't seem to mind the youngest Westenra. "To be perfectly frank," the young man continued, "I'm not looking forward to this conference at all. It's just another meeting to see what we can get from the Far East without giving anything back. Not that we should just let the Russians have it, of course, but there it is. I was never good at this diplomacy thing, in any event. Wanted to be a writer, but Father wouldn't hear of it."

He seemed almost pathetically glad to have someone to talk to. I suppose I couldn't blame him. With a family like his, it was probably difficult to have the slightest of meaningful conversations. This was proven just a few seconds later when the door flew open and Alexander burst in.

"Appleby! We're going to have to redo the entire seating arrangements! Nayland Smith just cancelled and—what, are you finally up, Peter? Another bender last night? Why am I not surprised?" He shook his head in contempt. "It's not like I haven't tried to help, Heaven knows. All the women I introduced you to in India. Hell, I even dragged you to a couple of whorehouses, and you know how easy Woggie women are. But no. Still, try at least not to embarrass us at the conference tomorrow, hm? Act like a man for just one night?"

"I'll try, Alexander," Peter said at last, voice low.

"I hope so. You know how important this is for my—er, Father's career. Oh, and Dickson—" He turned, putting the lowered head and red face of his brother completely out of his mind. "The rest of your crew should be arriving sometime around two. Give them the lay of the place and tell them to meet Sir Henry in the drawing room at four. He'll give you the rest of your orders then. You can handle that, can't you?" He swiveled back as if to go back into the main rooms, only to find his way blocked. For some reason Kritchna had risen and quietly placed himself directly in front of the door.

"Well? Out of the way, boy." There was a pregnant pause, then without a word the young Indian stepped aside.

As soon as Alexander had gone, he said, "Excuse me," and left via the servants' hall.

"I should go, too," murmured Peter.

Left alone in the kitchen, save for Mrs. Mulligan who made a great show of concentrating on the dishes. I tried to absorb all I had just learned.

Why had Kritchna so obviously placed himself in Alexander's way? I knew he hated the man, but that was grounds for dismissal. Was he trying to lose his position? And why was he condescending to work here in the first place? While his race foolishly and unfortunately barred him from many occupations, he was obviously too intelligent to stoop to mere Service. Even if the Westenras were too boorish in general to see it; surely someone in the Foreign Office would have noticed and snapped such a potentially valuable asset up. There was an undercurrent of something here; something I simply could not see.

And what was it that had killed poor Colleen? What had Kritchna had called the stuff again? Ectoplasm? I knew what that was—chemical mixtures used by fraudulent Spiritualists to make suckers think something came from "Beyond." My own father had used to concoct cauldrons of the stuff for his performances.

I thought of the upcoming séance at Rutherford Grange. Did that have something to do with it? Had Miss Annunciata been trying to play some sort of prank on us? I smiled grimly. She was a beautiful woman, but was no more a psychic than Roger Rutherford was a real werewolf, no matter what the superstitious peasants of the 17th century had believed. Spiritualism was all rubbish! Rubbish!

CHAPTER FIVE

The rest of the day passed uneventfully as I made a concerted effort to keep my mind on my official duties. I did not see Kritchna for the rest of the day. I was concerned, but decided that, whatever was happening, he should handle it. I had no right to press into his personal affairs, and besides had more pressing matters to attend to.

As Alexander had stated, the rest of the conference's security force arrived at about two o'clock. We gathered for a brief discussion, and I found them much as Mr. Blake had predicted. Good-hearted, eager to please, and bovine. Clearly, I would get nowhere with them. If anything truly bad were to happen, I would be on my own.

Kritchna reappeared at dinner, making no comment on his odd behavior, and I did not pry. Once again, we bunked together in his garret (now clean with fresh linen) but only made small talk.

The night passed without incident, and bright and early the next morning I rose, put on the fine suit Sir Henry had lent me, and went downstairs to watch the official guests arrive.

For all his haranguing, Sir Henry's rules for our behavior were quite simple. Keep quiet, do not speak to anyone of the least importance, keep out of the way, and, above all, do not touch the food. The others smiled and nodded like eager puppies, caring only for the wages at the end of the weekend. I simply stated I would endeavor to satisfy.

Sir Henry stated that remained to be seen.

As per my instructions, I hung back in a little alcove off the Great Hall as the officials arrived, mentally checking each one off as they came. There was Hale, usually connected with China but brought in from previous experiences in India. D'Athys, well-known explorer of Indochina. Ingles, the writer. A dozen others, all with their hordes of faceless assistants. They milled about, smiling, joking, and renewing old acquaintances though the formal introductions would not come until dinner. And then, at the end, the most important and famous of all. The Duc d'Origny.

He must have been an astoundingly handsome man in his youth; now age had faded that somewhat but even so, he carried himself with an air of poise and dignity many of his much younger compatriots could not meet. But it was neither cold nor self-important; his was the confidence of a man comfortable with both his strengths and flaws, a man who knew what he was capable of but who was not afraid to laugh at himself. The Duc d'Origny neither wanted nor needed any prestige, and it was that, more than anything, that made him such a natural leader. He accepted Sir Henry's gushing posturing with good grace; instantly recognizing that here was a weak man with little to offer, but willing to suffer him for a while for the greater good. Still, it was a surprise when he caught a glimpse of me out of the corner of his eye and instantly diverted his steps to come and shake my hand.

"The Duc d'Origny, young fellow. And you are?"

If my eyes were raised, Sir Henry's were practically bulging. Any more and his optic nerves would rip themselves out. Still, my mother had raised me to be honest. "Harry Dickson, Your Grace. I'm afraid I'm not a guest, just a security officer."

"There's nothing 'just' about it, young man," the Duc replied in his perfect English. "Every position is an important one in some way or other, and nothing to be in the least shamed over. Remember that. And now, Sir Henry, you were saying something about my quarters?" He smiled again, turned and rejoined his host, who by this time was suffering from massive eyestrain. I couldn't help but grin. This was going to be an interesting conference after all.

I had no idea.

The dinner was finished, the brandy and cigars broken out, and the guests shuffled slowly out of the dining room into the main hall. The hired musicians started up their instruments as Appleby and the other servants, dressed in their best, moved in unobtrusive grace among the crowd, refilling glasses and ready to answer every need. About them the guests mingled, sipping their brandies, chatting blandly about general politics, the weather and other such mundanities. The real discussions would not begin until the morrow. This was merely an after-dinner party, not the conference proper.

I hung back a reasonable distance from the main crowd, keeping a sharp eye on the proceedings. So far, all had gone well, if you discounted the fact most of the rest of the "security" had been surreptitiously helping themselves to the liqueurs for quite some time now. A few were just teetering out now to go on "patrol." I sighed. It was so hard to find good help these days.

Among the crowd, I noticed Kritchna; the handsome Indian cutting a striking figure in his finery. Not that anyone was paying much attention to him. He was merely a servant, and a Hindu at that. The fact that they were there to discuss the future of his own homeland mattered not one jot. Still, I couldn't help but wonder why some young maid back in Bombay hadn't snapped him up while he was still there. I was supremely grateful when he sidled up to me, casually handed me a brandy and said, "You look as bored as I feel."

"Worse," I replied, sipping the drink. "I need a smoke. But Sir Henry made it clear we mere detectives were to keep out of the way and not have any fun at all. Not that it's stopped any of the others."

"True," Kritchna grinned. "Two of them have been taking turns kneeling on the floor of the loo since the brandy came out. But if you insist on doing something on the cheap, you get what you pay for. Present company excepted, of course."

"Of course," I smiled. "Have you seen the Duc yet, by the way?"

"As a matter of fact, he actually spoke to me for a few minutes. I was giving him a drink and he insisted on asking me what part of India I was from, what I thought of the Russian threat and so on. Charming man. If only half the rest of these were like him rather than the host. And look, there's the Great Man now, lording over his court." He nodded toward the center of the room, and, sure enough, there stood Sir Henry, pontificating to anyone within earshot of the sorry state of Empire and how the Lower Classes didn't know their places anymore. At his right hand waited Alexander, nodding at whatever his father had to say, while a few paces back stood Peter, shuffling his feet and looking like he very much didn't want to be there.

"Well, I'd better get back to the guests," Kritchna said. "But, gad, this is tedious. I'd almost rather be at that séance they're holding at the Grange. At least, it would have to be more interesting than this."

"Please," I rolled my eyes.

"Not interested?"

"Kritchna, several years ago, my father was approached by a man. This man showed him a frog. He said this frog had the ability to put on a little top hat and sing ragtime. Truly. So my father watched and waited, and needless to say, all that frog did was sit there and croak. And that's all the dead can do. Sit there and croak."

Kritchna snickered. "All right, Dickson, all right. You sound just like my own father—eh?" His head swiveled toward the front door. Nor was his the only one. A sudden hush had fallen over the entire crowd and everyone was turning to stare at the new arrival who had just stepped majestically into the foyer, closing the door behind him. A tall, erect figure, radiating self-importance, who gazed out calmly at the crowd with the slightest glint of amusement in his eyes. A figure who had definitely not been invited.

I knew, for I had made a point of going over photographs of every one of the official guests. None even approached the appearance of this man. Tall, as I said, with a patrician, hawk-like face that held an air of dignity and intelligence I had seen in few others. His features were decidedly European in origin, but with his darkly tanned skin, as bronzed as Roxton's, his neat, immaculately groomed beard and spotless white turban resting comfortably upon his dark hair, he would've passed easily for an Arab or Sikh. Nor was this his only concession to the East. While his suit was European in fashion, and of the finest cut, around his waist rested a long, multicolored kilt-like garment I would later learn was called a *lungi*, a decoration from India. The combination of attires was jarring enough in this sea of cummerbunds and tuxedos, but there was something else, an aura of knowledge and dominance about the man that was unnerving. At his feet rested a large, perfectly ordinary carpetbag.

"I truly apologize for disturbing your soirée," he stated in a pleasant voice, "but no one answered the door so I was obliged to let myself in. Tell me, does anyone know if the Duc d'Origny is present? I just endured a most tedious train ride to get here and would like to see him."

Kritchna leaned close to me, frowning. "So who thinks he's Doctor Mystery, then?"

"I don't know," I grunted, "but he's about to leave." I began roughly pushing my way through the throng. Sir Henry would roll someone's head over this, and damned if it was going to be mine. Murmurings were already shooting up and down the gathering: "Who is that? Some damned woggie lover, I suppose." Still, none were making the first move to confront him.

It was Appleby who reached him first. For a moment it looked as if the butler was about to say something, but the stranger smilingly a card with a flourish and handed it to him. Appleby peered at it curiously a moment, then, in an uncertain voice, announced, "The, ah, Sâr Dubnotal. The Great Psychagogue, Napoleon of the Intangible and Conqueror of the Invisible!"

The Sâr Dubnotal?

Good Lord!

What on earth was that pretender doing here? Shouldn't he be at Grange, if anywhere? I had to get him out of here, and quickly. "All right, sir," I started as I reached him, "kindly explain yourself and why you have just intruded into a private conference..." I stopped in my tracks. For as I spoke, the patrician features had turned to me and I had to take a step back

His eyes. They were the deepest I have ever seen, glinting like sunlight on water, yet dark, boring, hypnotic, locking onto yours as drawing you in until you feared you would be lost in them forever.

"I never explain myself, young man," he said to me calmly. "It's entirely unnecessary. Suffice to say that I am the Sâr Dubnotal and that I am here." His smile grew broader. He didn't seem angry, just that his very presence should answer everything. It didn't, of course, and I was about to tell him so when I was interrupted:

"Doctor! Doctor, is that you?"

Immediately, the Sâr had turned his back to us, throwing out his arms in welcome. "Michel! My dear dear friend!" And he was embracing none other than the Duc d'Origny as if he were a long-lost brother!

"Doctor!" the Duc exclaimed, hugging the new arrival with the greatest of enthusiasm. "How long has it been?"

"Six years, ever since our adventure at the Devil's Gate, old friend! Far too long! How are you?"

"Fine! Whatever are you doing here? Were you invited?"

"No, no—I was in London visiting a friend on Cheyne Walk. We were interviewing an archaeologist about some very interesting occurrences on the Siberian Express a few years ago. But when Gianetti called and told me you'd be here, I just had to drop everything and come and see you!"

"Well, I for one am delighted that you did! It has indeed been far too long! Oh, yes; might I present M. Dickson? He has the honor of heading security for the conference." He gestured kindly toward me.

"Yes," the Sâr beamed, giving a slight bow. "My assistant told me I might have the pleasure of meeting you. The Rational Skeptic." He made an amused little clucking sound in his throat. Clearly he had met "Rational Skeptics" before.

This irked me more than a little, so despite the presence of the Duc, I flushed and responded hotly, "I am, sir. And proud of it. It was the Rational Skeptics that made the advances that pulled the world out of the Dark Ages, not those who claimed to follow the guidance of so-called 'spirits' and ended up dragging themselves and everyone who would listen into the black pit of superstition and occultic nonsense."

"Such as myself, of course." The Sâr's smile didn't fade.

"Yes." Every eye in the Hall was upon me, but I ignored them, turning instead to the Duc. "I sincerely apologize, Your Grace, if this man is indeed an old friend of yours. But I will not have myself or the teachings of my mentor spoken down to by anyone who fancies himself the 'Conqueror of the Invisible.'" I wheeled back toward the Sâr, daring him to reply.

Instead, he burst out laughing. "Excellent, Dickson, excellent!" he clapped his hands. "Well-spoken, indeed! Shake hands, sir; I'm glad to know you!" Before I could protest, he was pumping my right hand vigorously. "I see Gianetti did not lie when she spoke so highly of your spirit! And I'm certain Michel takes no offense, do you, Michel? Indeed, I find it an absolute pleasure to meet such a determined unbeliever in the Ab-Normal. As, I can plainly see, you are as well, sir." He glanced toward Appleby.

"I?" The butler frowned. "With respect, Sir, I am a follower of the Lord Jesus Christ. I refuse to have any truck with such satanic claptrap as the raising of spirits."

"A wise decision. The raising of spirits is a far more dangerous prospect that most who follow its tenets believe." His eyes flicked pointedly toward me "Nevertheless, you are correct for the most part, Dickson. At least ninety-nine percent of so-called 'occult phenomena' is merely the product of deluded minds or intentional chicanery."

"Naturally," I heard myself agreeing.

The Sar smiled. "Excellent. Then you would also agree that is that remaining one percent that makes all the difference."

"Mr. Dickson," the Duc suddenly put in, "I can guess how odd my friend's methods must seem to you. But believe me when I say they work. With this man I have seen... wonders. And terrors. He does not boast when he says there is more out there than Man can fathom."

I sighed. This was getting out of hand. "Be that as it may, Your Grace. But the fact remains I have a duty and this man is a trespasser at a sensitive Government Conference. As you vouch for him, something may be done, but otherwise I am afraid I must ask him to leave before—"

"Dick-Sonnn!!!!"

That happens, I thought miserably.

The roaring, rotund form of Sir Henry Westenra loomed over us like a just-awakened bear while everyone else in the area quickly turned their heads and started making their way to the far sides of the hall. His face, to put it mildly, was apoplectic. Alexander, ubiquitous as ever, hovered at his father's side as he roared,

"What kind of security do you call this, Dickson? Who is this man? How did he get in, and why hasn't he been removed?"

He made as if to physically grab at the Sâr. But the tall, regal man turned his eyes right upon him. In an incredible moment that seemed impossible to believe, the Sar's would-be accoster suddenly froze beneath the deep, sheer intensity of that gaze.

"I realize that I arrived here without an invitation, Sir Henry," the Sâr began in a cool, quiet voice. "But I was certain my dear friend the Duc would speak up for me. My actions were admittedly rude and I apologize for them; but I have not met my friend here in so long I simply could not pass up the opportunity to reacquaint myself with him."

Sir Henry's eyes flashed from the Sâr to the Duc, from the Duc to me, and back again

"I concur, Sir Henry," the Duc put in. "My friend the Sar here has never been known for his tact, but I would stake my life on him. I give you my word he intends no harm toward this conference. Therefore, you may do one of two things. You can welcome him as my personal guest, at my responsibility, or you may continue to look like a complete and total jackanapes in front of your guests." He gazed at Westenra steadily.

The Duc's words seemed not only to break the spell over Sir Henry, but deflate him as well. "I...see, Your Grace," he stated at last. "Please, forgive me. Certainly, if you recommend him I would be... glad to have this gentleman here for the evening. In fact, why don't you go out into the gardens and talk there? It's lovely and quite private. Alexander can show you where it is." He nodded toward his son, and, as if by a prearranged sig-

95

nal, the younger put his arm around the Duc, guiding him away. "Right this way, Your Grace."

"But I would rather—"

"Oh, it's no trouble at all, Your Grace." And they were out of earshot.

Very, very slowly, Sir Henry turned back toward us. "We. Shall. Speak Of This. Later." And he stalked away, pulling Appleby with him.

"Well, young Dickson" said the Sâr, "it seems my presence has gotten you in a bit of a jam."

"Oh, you think so?"

"Please try to retain your temper, young man. As it happens, I've had occasion to meet your Baker Street mentor a time or two. We don't really get on, for obvious reasons, but I'm sure that he'd be willing to listen to me. But who is this?" He glanced behind me.

Kritchna was waiting there, regarding the proceedings with a wry eye. "So you haven't thrown Prince Zaleski out yet?"

The stranger snorted. "Zaleski? That decadent layabout? I am the Sâr Dubnotal, young man;

'El Tebib' if you know Arabic, or simply 'Doctor' if you prefer. I take it you're one of the servants, and a most impertinent one." Suddenly he smiled, a flash of perfect white teeth. "I like that." Then, as he peered intently at the young Indian, the smile turned upside down. "Tell me, young man—are you at all psychic?"

"Me?" Kritchna's eyes rose at the unexpected question. "Psychic? Are you mad?"

"Certainly not," The Doctor's eyes probed the servant up and down intensely. "But your aura is one of the strongest I've ever seen. It's…well, it is *intense*. I have only seen the like a few times—with my assistant, with the most ascetic of Tibetan monks; and with my fellow countryman, Solange Fontaine. Oh, and the Figalillys, but they're so fey."

Kritchna frowned. Yet I felt his expression stemmed more from the sense of discomfort than annoyance. "I'm afraid I have no idea what you're talking about."

"Really?" The Sar seemed to lose interest. "Well, never mind. As I said, I'm merely here to see my friend; nothing more."

"Nothing?" I asked. "So you are not here to attend the séance at Rutherford Grange?"

He gazed at me sardonically. "Not in the least. That whole affair *does* smell of pure fakery, and my assistant is more than capable of exposing that. No, I am simply here to—"

But what he might have said next, we would never learn. For, suddenly, the air was rent with the most horrified scream of shock and pain I have ever heard. It screeched through the room like a sharp, keening knife, sending cold, spiky shudders down the spine of everyone who heard. Then it was gone—cut off as quickly as it had come.

The crowed stood frozen in stunned silence. The scream had come from the gardens. And now came another sound—a long, loud, mournful howl, as if from the throats of a dozen dogs. It hung like a dirge over us and ended in a crescendo of snarls.

"Michel!" the Sâr cried.

That was all I needed to hear. I tore through the crowd toward the garden doors, shoving my way past servants and diplomats alike. A mere half-pace behind me dashed the Sâr, gripping his carpetbag. For him, the crowd parted like the Red Sea. But no sooner had he passed than they immediately fell in behind him, trooping for the garden.

I pulled the glass-enclosed doors open with a mighty yank, my shoes clattering over the cobblestones of the walk. The Doctor was but a step behind. He very nearly collided with me as I stopped short, unable to believe what I was seeing.

"My God!" I heard a voice exclaim in a quaver—and was astonished to realize it was my own. For was what waiting before me was a scene of sheer impossibility

Alexander Westenra lay flat on his back, head bloody from a gash in his forehead, desperately trying to crawl backwards from the horror looming over him. Half a yard away upon the grass the body of the Duc d'Origny lay, sightless eyes bulging; a mass of red flesh and bone jutting out from where his throat had been. And, bent over Alexander in a bent parody of human posture, claws and teeth dripping with crimson, stood a garish figure I could scarce believe.

It was a wolf.

CHAPTER SIX

Yes; a wolf: a wolf fully seven feet high at the shoulder, black-furred, eyes glowing redly, shimmering with power and muscle. A wolf looming upright—upright!—on its hind legs, legs that ended in long, splayed feet like that of a distorted kangaroo's, reaching out its forelimbs toward the elder Westenra scion greedily. Paws too large, too thick; they looked more like the three-fingered hand of a some fur-covered giant.

And it was laughing.

Yes; laughing, a deep, rumbling, from the center of the torso chortle of malicious glee: "*Hree ree ree ree...*" It stepped forward, clumsily, as if uncertain of its balance. With each step there was a peculiar sucking sound, like water sloshing in a paper bag.

Instantly, I knew what had killed Colleen two nights before.

"Lord save us!" screamed a voice I recognized as Appleby's. "It's the Werewolf! The Werewolf of Rutherford Grange!"

Impossible, I thought automatically. What was standing before us, salivating blood and foam from its jaws, could not possibly be the legendary Werewolf of Rutherford Grange. Because werewolves simply did not exist. *Werewolves did not exist!*

If so, someone should have told the terror bending over Alexander Westenra. It threw back its head and howled, a bellow filled with hate and malice. With a little hop, it advanced before the cringing man. Then with a ravenous snarl, it sprang—

—And something rushed past me with the velocity of an exploding volcano, literally launching itself into the air to pound itself right in the center of the creature's chest, knocking it off its already precarious balance and causing both of them to fly backwards, skidding across the hard cobble.

For a moment, the Beast actually looked surprised. But it had no time to digest what had happened for now its attacker was furiously beating it across the face and snout with a fireplace poker it had seized, slamming the black bar against it again and again

"*No!*" Darshan Kritchna roared.

"Darshan!" I cried, the shock of what I was seeing freeing me from my temporary immobility. I dashed forward, not thinking of the danger, just knowing I had to do something, when the Beast—for I can call it nothing else—screeched and with a mighty heave of a powerful arm, swatted the man away like a gnat. Kritchna flew back, colliding with a set of patio chairs. He rolled over, groaning, and lay still.

The Beast was already back upon its feet, snarling, and shot a hand-paw out toward me. I felt myself hoisted off my feet and then everything turned on its head as I found myself hurtling through the air to land right upon a panicked Alexander Westenra. I was only able to extricate myself when a hand grabbed me by the collar and pulled; Peter Westenra had seized his brother and myself and was desperately trying to haul us to safety.

Everywhere else, pandemonium was ensuing, as diplomats, servants, aides, musicians and everyone else screamed and headed for the doors, shoving, cursing, trying to push their ways inside before the monster could charge them.

"Alexander!" screamed Sir Henry and shoved his other son away to grab at his eldest boy. A thick foot landed on my chest as he pulled Alexander to safety. Unseen, Peter quickly joined them. But the Sâr was moving forward; at the first sight of the creature, he had dropped to his knee, grabbing his carpetbag, and tore it open to pull out what looked like—Good Heavens! Some sort of semi-large, vaguely star-shaped stone. What did he plan to do with that, bung the creature with it?

He thrust out the stone, arm straight, and for a moment I actually had the ludicrous thought of a priest, shoving out a crucifix to ward off some evil spirit. Carved or painted into the star-like rock, I could see some sort of drab, rune-like sketchings the Sar faced directly at the Beast. From his mouth flowed a torrent of strange words, in a tongue I could not identify.

The Beast stopped dead in its tracks. In the Sâr's hand, the Stone almost seemed to glow—but it had to have been a trick of my blurry vision and the moonlight. "*Isha Thar Ch'taad!*" the man seemed to be saying, and the Beast pulled back. But then it struck out, arm moving like lightning, sending the stone from the Sâr's hand skittering over the cobbles and the Sâr himself into the lawn. Shaking as if in pain, it whipped around to find any other threats.

He found Mr. Appleby.

It was something I would never have imagined of him, but somewhere in the portly frame of the butler was a wellspring of courage previously unsuspected. He darted between the Beast and his masters, making the Sign of the Cross in the air and screaming, "In the name of God, *begone!*"

At the words, the Beast flinched, as if having been struck, lightly. It paused for only a moment, then the massive jaws split into a skeletal grin and it thrust its teeth for the servant's throat. Appleby fell over, tripped by his own feet, just in time. "Lord Jesus help me!"

Once again the Beast dropped back a bit, as if in some pain. Struggling to rise, still smarting from my blow, I tried to clear my head enough to think. Why was the Beast pausing? At Appleby's pleas? But those were merely words—weren't they? And what had the Sâr been thinking of?

Whatever it was, Appleby's delay gave the Doctor enough time to roll for the odd star-shaped stone again. Sweeping it up, he shot to his feet in a fluid movement, thrust it out once again and cried: "*Ch'nan vykos Nodens ka!*" Whatever that meant. And, in almost the same breath, "Do it again, man! The prayers! Say the prayers!"

For a dazed moment, I wondered whom he was yelling to, but then Appleby started again with the pleas to his God: "Our Father, Who Art in Heaven, Hallow'd Be Thy Name..."

Simultaneously, the Sâr advanced quickly upon the Beast, shouting out in his unintelligible tongue.

The Beast stopped, roared, and began to tremble violently. Caught between the two "chanters," it trembled like a cord strung between batteries—or so the thought came to my mind. It staggered, swaying drunkenly upon its legs, and for a moment, it seemed as if the fur and muscle of the creature was actually shimmering. Then it twisted, dropping upon all fours, and darted away across the lawn for the wall separating the estate from the outside world.

With one spring, it shot into the air, clearing the top with inches to spare, and vanished down the other side—and the wall was a good ten feet in height. Then there came one long, last howl—and it was gone.

It seemed an eternity before anyone moved. Then like a wave it hit, voices everywhere at once going: "God, what was that thing?" "A monster!" "The Duc! The poor Duc!" "What if it comes back? We've got to get out of here!"

In the midst of the crowd, Alexander was mopping his brow. "We had just come out to the garden when that thing leaped over the wall! Before either of us could move, it grabbed the Duc and tore his throat out right in front of me! Then it came for me! Me! I just thank God I'm alive!"

Sir Henry patted his shoulder. "There, son, you're safe now. I saved you."

Kritchna and I slowly picked ourselves up, heads aching. We looked at each other, daring the other to speak first. "Why?" I said at last, knowing full well he would understand my meaning.

The young Indian looked me straight in the eye. "Because that bastard's life belongs to me."

The Sâr had risen and carefully picked up his star-stone, looking out in the direction the creature had gone. "Is there anything in the direction the creature went?" he asked quietly.

"Rutherford Grange," replied Kritchna.

The Sâr said nothing. He pocketed the stone and went to the prone body of the Duc. Gently he knelt, cradling the staring head a moment. "My dear, dear friend." Then he gently closed the corpse's eyes.

"You!" The Doctor found Appleby standing over him. "What are you? A witch of some kind? A magician? Are you responsible for that—that thing?"

"Neither, and no," the Sâr snapped back. "What that Beast was and why it was here, I haven't the slightest. Yet. As for myself, I am merely a student of the Ancient Mysteries."

"A student of the Devil, more like! I saw you use that talisman!"

"I'll admit the Star-Stones have no particular link to Christianity. They represent other Powers. But *not* the Powers of Darkness—they were created to ward off evil, not strengthen it. You have nothing to fear from me, Man of God. The Powers I serve may not be exactly yours, but they are on the same side."

"That's impossible! There's only one God! I don't know who you are, but I know deviltry when I see it!"

"As do I," the Sâr gestured angrily. "And it just went over that wall. It's killed one of my dearest friends, it almost killed one of your masters, and if I don't get after it now, it will certainly kill again! If you cannot help me, Appleby, then kindly get out of my way! I must—here! Release me, sir!"

These last words were not said to Appleby but to Sir Henry, who had come up from behind him and seized the Sâr by the arm.

"You!" the master of Westenra House roared. "I don't know how you did it, but you've ruined everything! This didn't happen until you arrived! Alexander! Peter! Hold this man until I figure out what to do! Everyone else, stop! Come back! Get the—no!—no Police! My career—I mean, everything here is too sensitive! We can't let this get out! Wait! And you—" With his other hand he grabbed my collar. "You were supposed to be running security here! What kind do you call this? Now a guest is dead from some damned animal and my son was nearly killed! How dare you? How dare you?" So furious was he that he began shaking me violently, and I was in no mood for it.

"Let go of me, Sir Henry."

"Why? What you are going to do, boy, tell your employer? Your former employer when I get through with him?"

Something poked the fat man in the neck. The tip of a fireplace poker. "He said to let go of him, Westenra," Kritchna said in a low, angry voice as he brandished the instrument. "Now."

"Darshan, stop!" Appleby cried.

"Not this time," Kritchna said coolly. "I've been wanting to do something like this to you for a long time, Sir Henry. And I will if you don't release Dickson. Immediately." He pressed a bit upon the skin for emphasis.

"What are you talking about?"

"Oh, don't tell me you don't know. You and Alexander—Appleby! Let go!" He tried to wrench the poker from the butler's grasp but the elder man held firm. "Stop this, Darshan, before it's too late!"

"It *is* too late," came a voice and Alexander grabbed the Indian about the waist, pulling him away from his father. Arrogantly, he tossed him to the ground. "What do you mean, you damnable woggie?"

"My sister!" snarled Kritchna staring up at the man. Blazing hatred shone in his eyes. "Ashanti!"

"Ashanti?" Alexander blinked. "Ashanti? Who—what, you mean that little whore from Bombay? She was your sister?"

"She was," spat the Indian, "And she was no whore. Ever. You seduced her. Like you did dozens of other girls. Then when you got her pregnant you threw her aside!"

Alexander snorted. "Please. That little incident? It wasn't my fault if the girl couldn't control herself around white men. And I certainly wasn't going to take responsibility for some little half-breed mulatto. I thought she lost the brat, anyway."

"Indeed she did." The Hindu's voice was cold.

Alexander shook his head, glancing in bemsuement at his father, his brother and the crowd who stood listening. "What?" he asked the latter. " I did nothing half of you haven't done before. She was just some Hindu girl. And you're going to stand there and let some pagan savage threaten me for it? For some woggie stillborn?"

"For more than that," growled Kritchna. "Much more. Oh, don't look so innocent. You know what else you did. The very day your family leaves to go back here, my sister disappears from Bombay! You killed her! I know you did! I've been looking for proof ever since I got here! What did you do to the body, drop it in the river?"

Now Alexander actually looked surprised. "What are you talking about? I never saw the bitch after I told her to get out. I suppose I should thank you for saving my life from that—that creature.

"But I won't. You; you idiots who call yourself Security—kindly throw these men out!"

Suddenly a dozen hands from everywhere had seized me and were dragging me away, through the House and out the front door, across the gardens toward the gate. I was vaguely aware of someone's voice— Peter's?—crying out in protest. But it was no good. The gate was flung open and I was shoved forward, to land entangled with Kritchna in an undignified heap beside the road. The gate slammed shut behind us.

For a few minutes, we just lay there, panting as the voices faded. Then, slowly, we rose

"Well," Kritchna said ironically, dusting himself off. "That could've gone better."

I hit him.

"What did you do that for?"

"Just what did you think you were up to, you imbecile? Were you just going to up and murder Alexander in his sleep? Is that it? For what, because you think he murdered your sister? Where's your proof?"

"I was looking for it!"

"So that's why you lied about going to the cinema. Let me guess, questioning the villagers to see if any of them knew anything? I thought so. Damn it, why didn't you just tell me your suspicions? I'm a detective! I could've helped!"

"Vengeance belongs to my family," Kritchna said without remorse.

"Well, you know what's going to happen now, don't you? Eventually Sir Henry is going to think *you* sent that—that whatever-it-was to kill his son!"

Kritchna's dark face fell. "Oh. I hadn't thought of that."

"Did you?"

"Send that thing? No. I don't even know what it was! Appleby was shouting something about a werewolf; did you hear? You don't possibly think—"

I finally paused, out of breath and my imagination and emotions exhausted. "I don't know," I said at last. "But I do know I've got to get you out of here. I honestly believe you were as surprised as I was about the appearance of that Beast, but it won't be long before they're coming after you for it. Now the only way to prove your innocence is to catch it."

"I'm so glad to hear you say that."

From out of the bushes along the road, the Sâr emerged, carting his carpetbag as always. "I have a friend to avenge, and could certainly use your help."

I glared at him suspiciously. "How'd you get out here?"

"If your attention hadn't been occupied getting yourself dismissed from your position, Dickson, you might have noticed my climbing over the wall during the melee."

"And how do we know *you* didn't have anything to do with this?"

The Doctor's eyes turned cold. "You don't. But if you don't want your friend there to end up in jail or worse, you have no choice but to trust me. Now, quickly, into the bushes! I hear cars coming!" Without preamble, he was shoving us into the rushes, and for some reason we let him. Just as we did so, the gates to Westenra House swung open and a parade of cars sailed out, as fast as their wheels would carry them. We were close enough to see some of the drivers' faces; they were the aides of many of the diplomats attending.

"Looks like the conference is over," whispered Kritchna. "Do you think they're getting the Police?"

I shook my head. "I doubt it. Try explaining what just happened to a country constable! No, if I know Westenra, he's going to do his damnedest to keep this whole thing quiet. Not that it will work. The guests are bound to tell their superiors. Then, God knows what will happen."

"But it gives us an edge, nonetheless," replied the Doctor. "A few hours, at any rate. Dickson—you mentioned the Werewolf of Rutherford Grange. Tell me about it, quickly." Without knowing why, I did so. At the end, the Sâr frowned. "I have never heard this legend. And while I am no expert on therianthropology, I know enough. We must get to this Grange at once. Kritchna, do you know the way?"

"Certainly."

"Then let us go. My assistant is there already—and I have a very ugly feeling about this."

Hastily but cautiously, we slipped along the rest of the wall through the shrubbery, pricking ourselves several times but not daring to speak. Once on the far side, the foliage ended into long, grassy fields along the road—and no cover. We would have to be extremely careful, and not just to avoid being found by the Westenras. This was the direction the Beast had gone.

"Do you think it's still out there?"

The Sâr smiled grimly. "I'm sure we'll find out."

We moved quickly down the road, keeping our senses peeled for any signs of pursuit. There was nothing. Apparently the Westenras were too busy simply trying to save their conference to waste time chasing us. The Moon was out, giving us an excellent view of our surroundings. So it was that, about a half-mile down, we first saw the burly figure draped limply across the middle of the path.

The Beast lay still, its sides slowly rising and falling, but otherwise it did not move. It appeared to be dying. Cautiously, the Doctor removed another Star-Stone from his voluminous bag. He held it out toward the creature, murmuring words I could not clearly hear, but the Beast made no attempt to rise. It stared at us with its red eyes, panting, the face bruised where Kritchna had struck it.

"How could this be?" I found myself whispering. "It's impossible."

"Many things in this world are 'impossible,' Dickson," the Sâr said quietly, "But they happen anyway."

"Should we kill it? Or run?" asked Kritchna nervously.

"Neither, I think. If it could've attacked us, it would've by now. It's hurt. The problem is; I do not know why. This is most peculiar. The Star-Stone and the Incantations of Nodens should be drawing the curse out of this poor man, not physically harming him. He should've become human again by now." He paused. "In fact, it should have worked the first time back at the House. Why didn't it? They were clearly affecting it, but not as they should have. The only time this poor creature actually seemed truly struck was when both Appleby and I worked together."

"That reminds me," I said, "just how was all this supposed to work? Appleby was praying. Does that mean there's really a—"

"Not necessarily, Dickson," the Sâr said. "But what Appleby has is faith. That is great power in and of itself. Faith really does move mountains, you know. Sometimes it doesn't even really matter if the thing you believe in exists or not."

"He certainly didn't take to you afterwards," Kritchna pointed out.

"He was frightened and disturbed by what he could not understand. I don't blame him for that. But this is getting off the subject. We need to find out why this creature exists, and who it really is. Look! Something's happening."

The Beast raised its head and whimpered. All about it, from the tip of its toes to the tips of its ears, the entire

110

mass of fur and skin somehow seemed to be shifting. Flowing downward off the body like water.

Fangs dripped away into nothingness, skeletal structure and musculature ran off into pools of liquid upon the ground. It was incredible. This was not blood or any other bodily fluid, this was the body itself, turning into a thick, gooey substance that poured off itself, the form growing smaller and smaller as it did. With a shock, I realized I knew what the stuff was. It was the very goo I had found on the bushes beneath the garret two nights before.

"Ectoplasm," I heard the Sâr mutter. "This is unheard of."

For both of us, I thought. The head and snout had almost entirely melted away by now, slowly coming to reveal a wet mass of blond hair beneath the fur. Claws fell away, showing the long pink fingers of a woman. Chest and back fur slipped away into the remains of a crumbled blue dress. At last the full features of the person under the Beast became clear and I gasped in astonishment.

"Christina! Christina Rutherford!" I cried disbelievingly. "Christina Rutherford is a werewolf?"

CHAPTER SEVEN

The prone figure of Miss Christina Rutherford lay across the road before our stunned eyes; beautiful features marred by streaks of goo and thick bruises. Hair, skin and dress were sopping wet from the pouring away of the glop that had surrounded her—ectoplasm the Doctor called it—and her eyes, while open, stared blankly at us. Then it seemed as if recognition and memory all flowed back at once. Her mouth opened and she let out a howl, not of wolf-like malice and hatred, but one of terror, a long, drawn-out wail of horror and misery. She tried to rise but fell back, screaming: "Mama! Mama!"

To his credit, it was Kritchna who first knelt and gathered her up, pulling her close. "It's all right, Miss, it's all right. You're safe now"

"My God! Mother! Mama!"

"Miss Rutherford!" The Sâr gently took her from Kritchna. "My assistant, Gianetti. Where is she? Is she safe? What do you remember?"

"Gianetti?" She paused, not recognizing this man and unable to find the words to answer him. "I—I remember sitting at the table. Mama was there, and Uncle John, and Gianetti—and we were calling on Papa—and then—and then…"

"Go on," the Sâr said softly.

"And then…. and then, I felt hate. The most vicious hate. Coming over me."

"Hate? From within? Like something was invading your soul?"

"No…" Christina shook her head. "Like… like something from outside was covering me up, cocooning

me. And I saw Uncle John jump and Mama screamed…
and then I reached out for her but my hands weren't my
hands anymore—and I—and I—" She burst into tears.
"Mama!"

"Enough," Kritchna demanded. "Leave her alone."

"Someone's coming," I interjected.

The beams of headlights were flashing through the
night toward us, but not from the direction of Westenra
House—from the opposite, the direction of the Grange.
In an instant, a car which I recognized as the Rutherfords' own swerved toward us, screeching to a halt by
the side of the road, nearly banking into the ditch.

Lord John Roxton was out of the driver's seat before it was even fully braked. A rifle was slung over his
shoulder. "Christina! Thank God you've found her!"
Without preambles, he shoved the Sâr away to take his
niece in his arms. He looked haggard. "Christina, Christina, it is Uncle John. It's all right."

"Doctor!" cried another, and an equally-haggard
Gianetti Annunciata climbed out of the passenger side,
racing toward her mentor. "Doctor, what are you doing
here?" She seized his hands. He smiled down at her, in
evident relief, but if she would have liked more, he made
no move toward it.

"Gianetti, what has happened? Tell me everything!"

"Doctor, it's horrible! Mrs. Rutherford is dead!
Killed by that creature!"

"It's worse than that, my dear. It was here too. It
killed Michel."

"The Duc? He was killed too? Oh, sweet Mary."

"Doctor?" Roxton said. "Your employer's here?
My God! It's you!"

"Ah." The Doctor smiled, briefly. "Hello, Roxton."

"You're this 'Sâr Dubnotal' character? You? Back when I knew you in India, you called yourself—"

"No names, please." The Sâr held up a warning hand. "I left that identity behind a long time ago. For good reason. But the past isn't the issue right now. This young lady here is."

"You're right," Roxton replied. "In the car. We'll talk as we go. Christina, do you think you can walk? Let me help." Gently he placed his arm around the girl and assisted her to the vehicle. Gianetti took her other side. Gently, they set Christina into the passenger side, and Gianetti slid in beside her. Roxton looked at us, particularly the Sâr.

"Well, if you're coming, get in. This sounds like something you'd be involved in. Damn that séance!"

"Right," said the Sâr. "In!" Almost without thinking, Kritchna and I obediently piled into the back. The Sâr followed and the automobile revved into life, turning around and heading back the way it came.

"Uncle... Uncle John. Is Mama—"

"Shush, my dear. She's beyond any pain now."

Christina burst into fresh tears. Tenderly, Gianetti set her head upon her shoulder. "Don't hold it in. Just let it out!"

"Gianetti, I don't remember anything! Just—just that awful sense of hate. And then I felt myself change..."

"Enough!" The Doctor's voice was firm. "Explanations. Now."

"All right," Roxton said. "I take it you knew about the séance this evening? Damn it, I warned Althea not to have it! Not that I honestly thought anythin' like this would happen—I was afraid she'd be defrauded! You

know as well as I how many of these so-called Spiritualists are fake."

"And I daresay you thought Gianetti was, too."

"Well, I didn't know she worked for *you*, old lad!
Anyway, the other two—Grigori Yeltsin and Rosemary
Underwood—arrived right on schedule. We had dinner
and then Althea wanted to set the séance right up."

"Wait. Describe these other two mediums."

Now Gianetti spoke up. "I knew something was
wrong as soon as I met them, Doctor. Yeltsin—a very
fat, obnoxious man—claimed to be Russian, so I wondered why I had never heard of him, being as you take
such precautions to know what psychics are from there.
But I could see at a glance he was nothing but a fraud.
His aura was nil. Russian, yes, psychic, no. But Miss
Underwood... she was different. Her aura sang of power. Sang! I've never seen the like, except—well, except
in this young man here." She gestured toward Kritchna.
The Indian blinked, shifting uncomfortably. "His is almost as strong as hers. Very odd, too, considering how
drab she looks physically. Very plain, very colorless.
But there was something else about her I simply couldn't
put my finger on. Still, she seemed eager enough to help
Mrs. Rutherford, and I thought with my guidance, we
might be able to brush Yeltsin aside and actually summon Christina's father."

Finally, I found the words to speak. "But something
happened?"

Gianetti nodded, miserably. "The séance started according to plan. We had gathered around the table, link-
ing hands, and started the summons of Mr. Rutherford. I
was at the foot, Mrs. Rutherford was at the head, with
Christina next to her. Then, there was Yeltsin, and then
Lord John, and myself. We recruited two maids to help,

and then Miss Underwood was seated. I was keeping my best eye on Yeltsin. I expected him to try something. But then I felt the power."

The beautiful woman shook her head. "It was overwhelming, Doctor! But it wasn't like any other summoning I've ever done before! I—I can't describe it."

"Like the presence of an Outer Monstrosity?" the Sâr asked.

"No. Nothing so… alien. But hateful. Yes, something filled with hate. It swirled over us, like a great wind, and then…"

Lord John interrupted. "I would never have believed it. Even with all the two of us encountered back in India. But I was feeling it, too—something was actually coming. But it wasn't Althea's husband. I knew that, from the core of my being. It seemed to hover above us, like... I'm not certain, like it was trying to decide who to take. And then it fell. Fell right upon Christina. And then she changed."

"Changed. Changed into the lycanthrope?"

"Changed into something. Christina trembled and tried to cry out—and then suddenly it was like a shimmering halo had surrounded her, and she turned into that… that thing. Althea screamed. Christina was up, knocking over the table, and then she threw back her head and howled at us. Then, before any of us could move, she was reaching for her mother. Althea collapsed. The shock killed her instantly."

"That makes sense," the Sâr murmured softly. "The first impulse of the werewolf is to kill that which it loves best."

Gianetti cleared her throat. "Mrs. Rutherford wasn't the only victim," she said quietly. "We all panicked.

Yeltsin especially. Of course, the last thing he would ever expect would be something like this. He actually tried to run past the Beast. But the Beast... was quicker. Then it burst through the window to the outside, and from there... well, you already know what happened."

"And Miss Underwood?"

"Fainted, but unharmed. As are the two maids. They're terrified, but we persuaded them to stay and look after Miss Underwood until we got back. They're keeping themselves securely locked in the cellar."

"Doctor," Roxton said. "I know the story of the Werewolf. Everyone in these parts does. But I never believed it until now. Did we do it? Did we call up the spirit of Roger Rutherford by accident?"

"I don't know yet, John. A moment." He produced his Star-Stone mineral. "Miss Christina, please. I need you to hold this a moment. Yes, that's it. Now: do you feel anything strange? No shocks? Not even a tingle? Thank you. John, as soon as we get to the Grange, I need to do a complete examination of the scene. There's something very peculiar about this entire affair, and I want to find out what it is."

I feel so lost, I thought to myself, turning my head away to try and collect myself. In the past 20 minutes, my world had been stood on end. All my knowledge, all my training—right now, every bit of it seemed in vain. Psychics? Werewolves? Ghost werewolves? Murderers and kidnappers I could handle, but this!

"We're here," Lord John spoke, pulling the car to a halt. Peering over his shoulder, I got my first look at the infamous Rutherford Grange.

It was everything Westenra House wasn't.

Rutherford Grange hung back a little off the road, non-walled, non-gated, far more welcoming to strangers than Sir Henry's domicile. Much smaller, of course, with only two stories instead of three, and far less imposing, but nonetheless I could tell that it had been a grand farm in its day. The Rutherfords no longer planted, the fields being overrun by long grass and wildflowers, but the outbuildings were still there, worn but well-maintained, and I could hear a sheep bleat in the distance. The Rutherfords maintained a small flock and a couple of horses, but these were pets, not working beasts. Surrounding the house on all sides was a sea of colors: peonies and violets and a hundred and one other types of flowers everywhere, along the wall, in great clutches in the yard, around the great elms surrounding the house like welcoming parents; none planted to add to the aesthetic and proprietary value of the house but simply because they were lovely. Something stiff and proper martinet like Sir Henry would never think of.

The house itself was brick and Georgian—apparently the original building had burnt down years ago—and, like the surroundings, looked a bit shabby compared to its grander neighbor—some of the bricks were cracked and worn; the great green wisteria growing up to the roof was droopy, but all the same there was a sense of comfort here, a sense of belovedness. This was a home, not just a place someone lived in; a place where children played and laughter would not be hushed up lest the neighbors hear, a place where nobody cared too much if the cat scratched the furniture; a place where an old couple married for years still would sneak a kiss under the full Moon. The Rutherfords had influence and money, but refused to let it rule them. They preferred instead the better things; home, family, caring. The place practically rang of love.

And of tragedy.

A servant girl, haggard and frightened, opened the door. "Miss Christina!"

We gently moved our way inside and, despite the tragedy we knew was within, I found myself more and more impressed. The interior was by no means as fine as the House, or as fresh, being old and worn-down. But that was the wonderful part—this home looked used rather than simply existing; like people actually lived and loved and laughed here. Books weren't just set solemnly on the shelf, they were piled everywhere. Two or three cats moved among the furniture, mewing when they saw us. A large portrait of Mr. and Mrs. Rutherford hung over the mantel—but unlike the solitary Sir Henry, who stood alone, Mr. Rutherford had his arm about his wife as his other hand gently rested in both of hers. I liked this place. So it saddened me far more than perhaps it might when I found the two figures lying on divans, sheets drawn over both.

"Mother!" Christina made to draw the linens back from the smallest figure, but Roxton caught her hand. "Don't, my dear. It isn't pleasant." Christina sank to her knees and cried. Gianetti joined her there, placing her arms fully around the younger girl.

"Dickson," the Sâr said quietly, beckoning. I joined him as he carefully lifted the corner of the other sheet. I winced as I saw what had happened to Mr. Yeltsin.

"I don't recognize him," *El Tebib* muttered. "Not a Russian spy, then. Probably an Englishman using the name to make himself sound more exotic." He dropped the sheet. "Lord John, can you take me to where the séance was held?"

The Dining Room was shattered. What had been comfortable if worn chairs had been dashed against the walls, jarred to pieces. China dishes, which had been previously lining the walls, were cracked or broken entirely, tinkling down to the floor with dull clinks Something had lifted the main table and hurled it aside, bringing it down upon its flat. And what looked as if it had used to be a tablecloth was tossed ripped and crumpled in a corner. The edges were wet and crimson.

Two maids were there, trying to clean the place up as best they could, but there was someone else as well. This one was being watched over by what I assumed to be the butler, who gathered the maids and left when Lord John motioned for them to go. She sat on a chair silently, hands folded, looking very small and plain in an ordinary grey dress, brown hair dull and lifeless as her eyes. Her nose seemed rather long for an Englishwoman's. She gazed up listlessly as we came in.

"Miss Underwood?"

The medium called Rosemary Underwood nodded. "Yes, that is I," she said in a dull, rather monotonous tone.

"I apologize for holding you here," Roxton said, "but it was necessary for all to stay until we found Christina."

"Is she all right?"

"For now. The... Beast is gone from her."

"Only for a while," Miss Underwood spoke softly. "It will be back. She has been possessed by an evil spirit, and we are all doomed while she walks."

"Oh, I hardly think so," the Sâr said, and the girl looked up in surprise. "Do you know me, Madam? I should think my name would be famous in your circle. I am the Sâr Dubnotal, Conqueror of the Invisible!"

"I... believe I may have heard of you," the girl said at last, after a long pause. "What do you want with me?"

"Tell me. Tell me everything that happened here."

"Well, it began when Mrs. Rutherford contacted me about attempting to summon the spirit of her late husband..." Miss Underwood told her story. Apparently, the drab young woman made her living from using her gifts as a medium, after having discovered them a few years back. She had established herself in a town not far from Wolfsbridge and spent most of her time doing much the same as she had this night. It seemed odd to me—most of the Spiritualists I had met over the years were far more colorful and confident than this shy, unassuming woman. They had to be—confidence tricksters, every last one.

"...But this time, something was different. I felt it. I thought it was because that Mr. Yeltsin was so obviously a nonbeliever. He was just in it for the money. But I felt Hate coming... vicious, enraged Hate. And then Miss Rutherford turned into that thing. The rest, you know." She shrugged. "Take my advice, Doctor. Leave here. Let us all leave here. There is no help for her now. She has become the Werewolf of Rutherford Grange, and her soul is lost."

"I respectfully disagree, Miss Underwood" the Sâr replied. "I'm no expert, but I know a bit about lycanthropy and other manifestations of it. The werewolf sightings in New York State in 1799, the infamous wolf and man-cat of Paris, the Serbian feline shape shifters... even the notorious Ring of the Borgias. I'm certain that, with a bit of investigation, I can find the solution to this. In fact, I'd appreciate it if such a talented psychic as yourself would care to assist me."

For the first time, a bit of color appeared in the girl's cheeks. "I'm afraid I can't," she started. "I must go at once. I have no wish to deal with demons. It would be safer—"

"It would be safer if you stay here where we can protect you," Roxton declared firmly. "Trust me, Miss Underwood. I know this man. He knows what he is doing."

"Lord John." Darshan Kritchna stuck his face through the door. "Miss Christina is asking for you."

Automatically, we had turned to follow the sound of his voice. And that's when Miss Underwood chose to make her move. Darting up faster than any of us would have expected, she shot past me and made for the back door, which I could see through the kitchen

"Stop!" Roxton cried, and dashed after her. The last I saw was of a brown cloud of skirts being held up as the girl ran across the fields as fast as her legs could carry her.

Within a few moments Roxton came panting back in. "She's gone. I wouldn't think a woman could move so quickly, but—"

"Damn," I said. "I'll get the car; I should be able to catch up—"

The Sâr shook his head. "No, Roxton. Let her go. She can be no further help to us. We can find her if we need her again." Roxton looked dubious but the Sâr turned to Christina. "My dear, I realize this night you have experienced horrors unimaginable to the average person. But you must be strong for a little while yet. I need your help. For your own sake. But also for the sake of your mother, for the sake of my friend Michel—and for the sake of everyone else the Creature who took control of you threatens."

The girl gazed up at him with tearful eyes. He smiled down at her. Then, she swallowed, nodded her head, and said:

"I—I'll help in any way I can."

The Doctor's smile widened. Gently he placed a hand upon her shoulder.

"Your courage is great," he told her softly. "For that, you have my greatest admiration."

"What…what must I do?"

"In truth? I need you to make a telephone call for me."

Ten minutes later, the doorbell rang. Christina, still sniffling, opened it.

"Miss Rutherford!" Appleby cried in concern. "Whatever is the matter? Why did you ask me to come?"

"We—we need your help, Mr. Appleby."

"With all due respect, I cannot possibly see what I can do for you what your own servants could not. Sir Henry will be furious—"

The Sâr gripped him by the arm and yanked him inside. Before the butler could protest, he had clamped one hand over his mouth and was peering intently into his eyes.

"Appleby, listen to me. I know your beliefs. I'm not asking you to change them. I know how frightened you are of all this. And you should be—working with the Spirits is always the most dangerous of propositions, no matter how experienced you are. But you know as well as I—there's a monster out there, Appleby. One that I believe is a threat to your masters. And if we're going to save them, I'm going to need your help. You may not like me. You may not like my methods. But believe me when I say our objectives are the same—to prevent a great evil from occurring here. When I take my hand from your mouth, if you still do not wish to help, I will not stop you. But I need you, Appleby. I need what you can give to us. So I ask—will you assist us? The answer is totally up to you."

The two stared into each others' eyes for a long time. Then, slowly, Appleby motioned for the Sâr to remove his hand. "Sir," he said quietly, "you are right that I believe your... views are not the correct ones. But I know what I saw tonight, and it was total Evil. Evil that must be fought. I will not use your methods for myself. But... if somehow I can call upon God to help you, I shall."

"That's all I wished to know, Appleby. Thank you. Now, quickly—what is happening at the House?"

"Sir Henry is in a frightful state. Mr. Alexander and Mr. Peter are too. All the guests have fled. No one even stayed to help with the body—I had to do that. We're keeping him in a side room, properly covered until Sir Henry can decide what to do."

"You mean he hasn't summoned the authorities?"

"No, sir—he is adamant about that. He wants no one from outside to know what happened. I'm not certain he has even informed the Government yet—I asked if he wished me to call the Office and he refused. But they must find out, and soon. The other diplomats are certain to inform their superiors."

"What about the rest of the security?" I demanded. "Where are they?"

"Gone, as well, sir—as are the rest of the servants. They're all too terrified to remain. I can't blame them. But Sir Henry cannot possibly intend to keep this whole thing a secret."

"He probably does," said the Sâr. "He's the type who would, just to salvage his career. But we have little time. The normal authorities cannot possibly handle something like this, even if they would believe it. If the spirit of the Werewolf of Rutherford Grange is truly about, we have to deal with it ourselves."

I folded my arms skeptically. "And just how do we find out if this is the real Werewolf?" I scoffed.

'Simple," the Sâr said calmly. "We're going to have to talk to the source of the legend himself."

"We're going to what?" My voice must have cracked with my incredulity. "Please, please, please tell me that you're joking."

"I never joke, young man," the Sâr replied flatly. He carried a chair to the far side of the room and set it down. "Not about this, at any rate. Here, Kritchna, help me with this table."

"But—but another séance!"

El Tebib glanced at me sardonically from beneath his turban. "Does the Prince of Rationality have a better idea?"

All about the destroyed dining room the Sâr and Miss Gianetti were rummaging about, moving chairs, picking up bric-a-brac, and sweeping debris from the center of the room to form a clearing in the rough shape of a circle, large enough for the six of us to stand around it, or sit if we scrunched. In the center of this clear area, the Sâr had been careful to remove the slightest bit of dust or dirt. He then opened his carpetbag and pulled out a gangly, shapeless mass of metal and wires. This he set within the circle and started to rearrange it, clicking together two bars here, untangling strands of wire there, until the whole thing came together and I realized that it was some sort of collapsible pentacle of some sort, but one which did not quite match the geometry of a perfect pentagram. The points seemed too curvy for one thing, and it was placed in such a way that the angles were not exactly compass-straight. The Doctor straightened up, looked at it, didn't seem satisfied, and shifted it slightly to the left. Then, apparently content, he unraveled of all things an ordinary extension cord and asked if anyone saw an outlet.

"One of Thomas's electric pentacles?" asked Gianetti.

"A variation of my own devising," the Sâr replied. "With Thomas's, the entity remains outside, while you are within. With this, we stay outside and it stays inside."

"A pentagram!" cried Appleby in something of a strained voice. "But you said—"

The Sâr held up a hand. "Be at peace, Appleby. Yes, it's a pentagram. I know the associations with Black Magic it holds. But there are reasons for that—it works. This shape applies to both White and Black Magic, and none of us who do battle with the more sinister aspects of the Ab-natural can do without it." Continuing to gaze upon the butler, he smiled gently and sympathetically placed a hand on his shoulder. "I know all too well what you're feeling, Appleby," he said, "I told you that I have never called upon the Infernal Powers for assistance, and I'm not about to start now. In my own way, I serve the same Powers as you. In fact, that's why I asked specifically for your assistance. You bring something very valuable to our project."

"And what might that be?"

The Sâr raised his eyebrow. "The power of faith," he said simply. "Faith is a far more powerful force than most realize. Especially faith in something greater and better than ourselves. That grants much protection against the forces of evil. They cannot face the idea of Faith."

"Oh, that makes no sense whatsoever!" I snapped. "If that is the case, then you could ward a vampire off with enough faith that the sky is blue!"

"You think so?" the Doctor asked. "I'll remember that the next time I encounter a vampire. But, seriously, Appleby, your presence is more necessary than you might think."

"Please, Mr. Appleby." Gianetti took his arm. "The Doctor is right. He would never ask you to do something so against your beliefs if it wasn't absolutely necessary. At one time, I didn't trust any of this, myself. Did you know I was actually going to become a nun? Oh, yes. I'm a very devout Catholic." Tenderly she fingered a rosary hung about her neck. "But I have a gift that, for whatever reason, I firmly believe God gave me. When it first manifested, I thought I was going insane or was possessed. And I nearly was. An evil woman named Madame Sara was trying to use me to call up—well; I don't want to talk about that. But if the Sâr hadn't found me and taught me how to use my ability properly, taught me how to use my own faith to channel my powers, let's just say something—bad—would have happened."

"Indeed," the Sâr exclaimed firmly. "The great difficulty here is that this place has already been used for evil, and that attracts more evil. It's only because Miss Annunciata's abilities are inborn to her, along with my own learning and devised defenses, that we have even a chance in succeeding in our mission. But succeed we must, if we are to stop even more deaths from occurring. Adding your own faith, as well as"—he nodded toward Kritchna—"this gentleman's innate psychic gifts, whether he wants to acknowledge them or not, I believe that, with caution, we stand a great chance of summoning the spirit of Roger Rutherford."

Appleby still looked skeptical, but I could tell the pleading face and gentle persuasion of the beautiful Miss Annunciata was winning him over. I shot a glance at Roxton, practically begging him to interfere. But the great adventurer simply shrugged in defeat. This had come too far and the Sâr had reminded him of too much he had seen over the years to back out now.

"Still," the Doctor said, "I will not force anyone to participate in this if they truly do not wish to. So, if you want to back out, now is the time. Gianetti?"

She shook her head. "You know I won't."

"Roxton?"

Lord John took a deep breath and sighed. "Lord if I understand all this," he said at last, "but if it will bring out that monster and avenge Althea I'm with you. But must Christina—"

"Hush, Uncle," the young woman said, stepping forward, face tear-stained and bruised, but very determined. "This... thing forced me to kill my own mother. Of course I'm in." She squeezed Gianetti's hand for strength. The elder woman was more than willing to give it.

The Doctor turned. "Mr. Appleby?" After a moment, the butler nodded. "I feel like Saul approaching the Witch of Endor," he said quietly. "But there is something evil here that must be stopped. And while I will not call upon your powers over my Savior, I will pray that He somehow chooses to reveal the truth here."

"You don't have to," the Sâr proclaimed. "Just ask for the Hand of Riathamus to be upon us as we embark upon this journey. Kritchna?"

The Indian simply nodded.

"And you, Dickson?"

Everyone's head turned toward me. I paused, unable to believe what I was doing here. No, I thought, no. This went against the grain of everything I was ever taught, everything I had ever trusted. There were always rational explanations for everything that happened. Everything. The supernatural simply did not exist.

But what if I were wrong?

If I was wrong—and I wasn't yet certain that I was—then, that Beast would still be out there, ready to kill at a moment's notice. And this might be the only way to stop it. So, in spite of myself, in spite of my mentor, in spite of everything I ever knew about the world, I found my mouth opening and these words issuing out: "I'll do it."

The Sâr nodded. For a moment I thought I saw in his eye a glint of admiration. "Good. Then everyone gather here at the edge of the circle. Join hands. Appleby, if you wish to pray, start now."

Quickly, he plugged in his contraption, which began to glow softly with a gentle blue electricity. Then he switched off the lights and squeezed between Kritchna and myself. "Gianetti will do the actual summoning. All the rest of us have to do is be still and think 'Roger Rutherford.'"

In the dark of the room, the pentacle's glow grew brighter. Out of the corner of my eye, I could see Roxton gently grasp his niece's hand more tightly. Gianetti began to mutter words under her breath. Her eyes had drawn back into themselves and she seemed to take no notice of where she was or whom she was with. Next to Kritchna, I could hear Appleby gently chant: "Our Father, Who Art in Heaven, Hallow'd be Thy Name…"

I swallowed silently. In the midst of the circle, the blue of the pentacle sparked and crackled in tiny pops. I tried to catch Kritchna's eye but he was staring intently into the middle of the circle. I did as well, but could make out nothing. Then, suddenly, Gianetti threw back her head and cried out at the top of her voice: "Roger Rutherford! Roger Rutherford! We ask you to come beyond the Winds of the Shadow to us to stop a great evil! Roger Rutherford! Are you there?"

And now, I paid more attention than ever. I knew all the tricks of the Spiritualist trade; every one of them. Trumpets used to throw voices. Special wires to lift tables. Everything. If the Sâr or Gianetti or anyone was up to trickery here, I would know of it. Swiftly, I glanced across the circle; everyone was still gripping each other's hands. Everyone's eyes were open and they were all looking into the clearing. Neither the Sâr nor Gianetti made any move.

Then, very slowly, there was another sputter of the pentacle and it seemed to throw off a blue spark. The spark flew upward, just over the top of the clearing, and paused, seeming to hang in the air itself. Then it expanded—expanded up and out, still hovering over the floor, but fleshing out to become a small, floating illumination that flickered and licked upwards like a tiny fire. I felt no heat from it, nor cold. It was simply there. I probed for any sign of a wick, a torch, an electric light, anything that might tell me where it was coming from. But I could see nothing. And then the voice came.

"*I... am... here.*"

"Roger Rutherford?"

"*Yes. I have... been allowed... to come.*"

("Allowed?" I heard Appleby whisper. "Allowed by whom?")

Quickly, I checked the Sâr. There was no movement of his lips, no pulsing of the throat that might indicate ventriloquism. But I had met professionals before. I kept my eye on him as Gianetti continued to speak:

"Do you know why we have summoned you?"

"*Yes. The Beast.*"

"Are you the Beast? Is it your ghost or the ghost of one of those hung with you?"

"*Difficult...to speak beyond the veil. Very... dangerous. But no... it is not. It is... something different. Something not... of this side.*"

"Then what is it?"

"*I cannot explain. It is not... of this side. That is... all I know.*"

"Were you ever the Werewolf of Rutherford Grange?"

"*No. I was... only a man. I did not... practice the occult. That is why I was allowed to come... to tell you.*"

"Then what was it?"

"*A gypsy beast... that escaped. Spotted and laughing. Fierce. It... hurt me. and I was taken for it. But only... a beast.*"

That matches what I read in the diary, I thought. Spotted and laughing—that sounded much like a hyena. Could the gypsies have brought a hyena with them and it escaped? That would certainly fit the description—a creature bigger than any dog anyone in the area had seen, very ferocious, and which would've "laughed" when they saw it! Almost certainly no one in Wolfsbridge would have ever seen one before—they were not stupid people, but with their lack of education, it certainly would've seemed like something supernatural! But then the thing I saw looked no more like a hyena than it did a real wolf.

Very quietly, the Sâr spoke. "Do you know who is responsible for this?"

"*You... already know.*"

"I believe I do." The Sâr nodded. "Thank you."

"*I... must go. Already the... dark dwellers approach. And the voice... calls me home. I... must go. But Christina... Christina Rutherford...*"

"Y—Yes?" the girl asked uncertainly as tears streaked down her face.

"*Your family told me... They love you. They love you... Christina.*"

She swallowed. "Tell them... Tell them I love them, too."

"*They know. The dwellers come. Good-bye. Good-bye...*"

"Wait!" Kritchna cried out, almost breaking his hold on the Sâr's hand and reaching out to the light. "I must know! My sister! My sister, Ashanti! Is she there? Is she there with you?"

There was a pause. Then:

"*She is not... On this side of the veil. That is all I know. The dwellers... Must go... Must go now...*"

The voice faded and the blue glow began to shrink. But in its place something else began to form. It began as a pinprick, just a sliver of blackness at the bottom of the blue, somehow seeming darker than the room itself. But it was growing swiftly, growing wider and stronger, seeming to absorb all light, even the light of the pentacle, and at the very core of my eardrums I heard a strange sound... a sound that seemed like the inane chattering of evil apes...

"*Pull out!*" cried the Sâr, tearing his hands from ours. "Gianetti, pull out *now*!"

With one heave, he yanked the cord from the wall. The illumination of the Pentacle instantly went out. Simultaneously, the cloudy "darkness" within the contraption suddenly seemed to withdraw into itself; vacuuming backwards into its own mass if, as it were, it were some kind of light-reversed candle snuffing itself out. Gianetti fell backwards; Lord John just barely managing to catch her. As for myself, I felt sweat beading down my face. This was...unlike anything I had ever experienced before. Throughout the entire sequence, I had been watching and peering, searching for any of the signs my father had taught me about dealing with the usual Spiritualist chicanery. Yet nothing had I found that smelled of a hoax. And that strange, evil chattering at the end...I found myself trembling and cursed myself for my foolishness. This could be explained, I thought. *This could be explained!*

I glanced toward Appleby. He was on his knees, audibly thanking God for saving us. The Sâr clapped a hand on his shoulder.

"You sensed them, didn't you?" he asked. "If it were not for you, the Dwellers in the Dark would certainly have interfered that much sooner. We were fortunate."

The butler shook his head. "Don't thank me, Sir. It is the Lord who should be thanked."

The corner of the Doctor's lips twitched. ""Indeed," he said simply and went to attend to his assistant. Gianetti was gently being helped up by Lord John.

Kritchna came over to me. His face was ashen and his voice low. "What do you think?" he asked in a whisper—a whisper I detected a distinct shudder within.

I remained silent a long moment. I hated what I was about to say. "I...don't know. I'm just... I'm just very, very confused."

"So am I. But somehow—somehow, I think that was real. Don't ask me how I know, I just feel it. In my bones. That's why I asked about my sister. At least now I know... she isn't dead."

Part of me wanted to cry out that she had to be; there was no way that was a true spirit called up; this was all some part of a terrible, terrible dream. But I heard my voice saying instead: "But if Alexander didn't kill her, where could she be?"

"I don't know."

With a swallow I finally dared look toward Christina. Tears were flowing freely down the girl's cheeks. *"They're all right,"* she whispered softly to herself. *"They truly are all right...."*

"Well, Doctor?" Roxton stood before the Sâr. "Did that little contretemps really solve anything?"

"Indeed it did, Lord John," the Sâr replied seriously. "I know precisely what we're dealing with now."

"And that would be?"

A grim smile played across the Sâr Dubnotal's lips. "Let me make one more telephone call. And then, you may wish to load your rifle."

CHAPTER EIGHT

During the next half-hour, we made our plans. The sun had risen by now, spreading its light into the gloom of the Grange. Under normal circumstances, the dawn was the most welcome of visitors to this house, but now it appeared a intrusive stranger. The Sâr had sent the servants away, with strict instructions not to speak to anyone, and assured them that Miss Christina was now free from any possession and that the Beast would be conquered. Not even my mentor could sound so convincing.

At one point, Kritchna noted the Doctor had apparently plugged the "Electric Pentacle" back up. The turbaned metaphysician told him to keep things as they were.

Breakfast was quick and muted; then the Sâr took Appleby into the kitchen to make the call. When they returned, the butler appeared quite uncomfortable. The Doctor, for his part, simply looked determined. He spoke in low tones with Roxton and Gianetti; then we all settled down to wait. Roxton had his rifle by his side.

Ten minutes later, a car pulled up outside. There was a furious knocking upon the door.

"Open it, Appleby," the Sâr Dubnotal said.

Nervously, the butler complied. Sir Henry and Alexander Westenra pounded in, red-faced and looking extremely tired. Sir Henry was already barking: "Damn it all, Appleby, you'd better have a good explanation of what you're doing here instead of at the House!" Then his eyes widened as he took in me, Kritchna, and above all, the Sâr. "What are you doing here? What is the meaning of this?"

135

"Sit down, if you please, Sir Henry." The Sâr gestured to a pair of empty chairs situated near the Pentacle.

"I most certainly do not please!" Sir Henry snorted. "I shall—"

"On the contrary," Lord John stated, shutting the door behind him and fingering his lifted rifle pointedly. "I think you will do quite what the Sar asked, Sir Henry."

Sir Henry and his son sat, looking from one to the other of us in confusion and irritation.

The Sâr regarded them solemnly, fingers steepled to his chin. "I'm aware you're both quite exhausted, gentlemen, as are we all. So I will endeavor to keep this as short as possible. You are, of course, perfectly aware of what happened to my old friend the Duc d'Origny at your estate last night. What you may not know is that this Beast was also here, where it slew Mrs. Althea Rutherford and one of the Spiritualists she was hosting."

"So it's true?" Alexander asked "They really did call up the spirit of the Werewolf Grange?"

"Nonsense," snapped Sir Henry. "It was just some creature this man bought to disrupt the conference. I know it!"

The Sâr paid him no mind. "Oh, they certainly called up something during the séance, there's no doubt about that. But if my theory is correct—and they are never wrong—it was by no means a ghost."

Now it was my turn to be surprised. "What? Then what was it?"

The Sâr frowned at me, disapproving of my interruption. He turned back to his unwelcome guests. "May I ask you a question, Mr. Alexander? During your time in India, you frequented many places, did you not? That is, places where an Englishman of your standing would

136

rather not be seen if he wanted to keep his reputation. I do not mean brothels and the like. I instead refer to other associations—such as those with certain Russian agents. And temples of certain cults the British authorities consider most dangerous. Please, please; calm yourself. Your past is no secret to those who frequent India. I've heard of your exploits, as has Lord John himself. Ah, but you were a reckless youth back then, weren't you? Always looking for amusement. You even made the acquaintances of several native women, or so I've heard." He glanced toward Kritchna, who was looking at the Westenras as a cobra does his prey.

Alexander Westenra glared. "Are you accusing me of treason, sir?"

"I am not. For we both know that your father was always there to pull you out before you fell into things too deeply; don't we? There is nothing so pure as a father's love, is there? Still... you may have heard of a few things when you were associating with the darker magicians and occult masters you enjoyed so much. Such as, for instance, the term *tulpa*. Have you?"

"Say again?"

"Oh, come now, Mr. Westenra. Surely you've heard of the *tulpa*. It's a very special thing in occult circles."

"No."

"No? Truly? Then allow me to enlighten you.

"A *tulpa* is something very difficult to create. Very. Indeed, only the most learned or powerful of yogis even try. But if you succeed...then, you have created yourself a very powerful weapon. Very powerful, indeed. If, in fact, you can control it. That's quite hard. For, you see, the *tulpa* is a being created from the mind itself."

"What?" I was incredulous. "Now this is going too far!"

"Quiet, Dickson." Lord John said quietly. "The Sâr is right. I've seen such things before."

"Too true," the Sâr replied. "In the Black Temple of Mongolia. But to resume: the *tulpa* is neither a ghost nor a natural spirit. It is pseudo-life: an animated creature, often in the form of a natural beast or person, created from ectoplasm by the imagination of the yogi. As I said, only a few people can create them. And far fewer can control them for any length of time. You see, they are intensely angry creatures—angry for they know that you are real and ultimately they are not. And they hate it. Hate it to the core of their pseudo-existence. Ideally, one should have experienced years of study and meditation before even attempting to create a *tulpa*—but it can be done by less trained psychics. Not very well… but it can be done."

By now Alexander was looking bored. "All right; yes, perhaps I recall hearing the word a time or two before. What does that have to do with anything?"

"Just this. The Werewolf who killed Mrs. Rutherford and my friend last night was no ghost. It was a *tulpa*."

Sir Henry took the cigar out of his mouth. "For God's sake—" but the Sâr continued.

"I first began to suspect when my Star-Stone didn't draw any curse out of poor Miss Rutherford here—yes, gentlemen, she was the 'werewolf,' but by no means of her own accord. When we found her in the road, surrounded by ectoplasm, I knew we weren't dealing with a true lycanthrope. The 'Werewolf' was in actuality a psychic shell surrounding the girl, not a physical transformation in and of itself. One that temporarily controlled her, but yet not strong enough to last permanently.

"No, Miss Christina was simply an instrument in someone else's hands."

"Then, who?" Kritchna asked.

"Ah." The Sar smiled. "Based on my previous experiences with *tulpas,* I immediately realized that it could not have been a very experienced psychic that formed it. Otherwise, the Werewolf would have existed and acted as its own form. But, no—whoever created it obviously needed some sort of base to form the ectoplasm around; an already-existing 'skeleton,' as it were, so the Beast could move and walk and do what its creator wanted it to."

The audience sat spellbound by the Doctor's words. So intent, in fact, that even Roxton had turned his attention away from his surroundings, leaning forward to catch every word. So he did not notice as I did when the drawing room door slowly and silently began to creak open.

"Look out!"

To his credit, Roxton was instantly alert and turning, bringing up his rifle to face whomever it may be, but the door burst open and the cold barrel of a pistol pointed directly toward his heart.

"Hold up there, Lord John, if you please," Peter Westenra said mildly. "Now, kindly lower the rifle to the floor... That's it. Thank you. Now, please, move over there with the others. Everyone else, kindly stand with your hands in the air. That means you as well, Doctor."

"Ah," the Sâr said calmly. "I must admit I wasn't expecting you to follow your elders, young man. Careless of me."

"So it was." He gestured with the pistol. "All of you, in one group, over there. But please do not think of rushing me, for I would hate to have to shoot one of the ladies. And I shall, if you try anything."

All of us, Appleby included, obeyed. Sir Henry heaved in relief. Even Alexander was impressed.

"Thank God, Peter!" he ejaculated. "Finally you ended up doing something right! Here, kick that rifle toward me, and we can—"

"Alexander," Peter stated calmly, pointing the pistol straight at him, "shut up." And he sent a bullet through his brother's head.

Christina screamed. Alexander Westenra, blood streaming from the hole in his forehead, teetered a moment, as if unable to quite process what was happening. Then he fell over, spreading crimson upon the carpet.

"Son!" cried Sir Henry and made to go to the body, but the pistol had swerved to cover him while its holder never took his eye off us.

"Get over there with the rest of them, Father. Now!"

"Peter Westenra, what the Hell are you—"

"Do it!!!" screamed Peter, finger tightening on the trigger. The look on his face was the antithesis of the sallow, sad expression I had known before. After a moment, unable to tear his eyes from the body on the floor, Sir Henry obeyed.

"I have to admit you surprised me on this one, young man," the Sâr said. "I honestly did believe it was your brother."

Peter smiled, bitterly. "The more fool you, then. Isn't it always the one who seems the meekest? To tell the truth, I'm the one who's surprised Dickson didn't figure it out—you're supposed to be the great detective, after all, aren't you> Ah, well—the truth never matches up to the fiction."

"Son!" Sir Henry cried, "What are you doing? "

"Oh, it's 'son,' now, Father? At long, long last? Please. You never paid any attention to me before, why start now? After all, I've only ever been an embarrassment to you. Because I was sickly and weak, and never came up to your standards of manliness. Kindness and compassion were always detriments to you." The pistol held steadily at us. "Well, congratulations! Years ago you finally burned all the compassion right out of me. Oh, I hid it well. I decided to. That way, you left me alone. And you never stopped to consider what I might really be getting into while in India."

"Of course," I said. "When Alexander took you around, trying to make a 'man' out of you. You must have met fakirs among the rest of the riff-raff he made you associate with. They taught you about *tulpas*."

"Oh, more than that. Much more. The problem was; I didn't have the innate talent to utilize any of it. None of us Westenras do. So, obviously, I needed to find someone who *did* possess such talent. And, lo and behold, she came to me. Would you like to meet her?" He dared a quick look toward the door. "Come on in, darling."

From the doorway, there was the sound of light footsteps, and a woman walked in. No one was surprised to see Rosemary Underwood, also holding a pistol. But we were when she reached up and yanked the drab brown wig off, revealing a long mass of luxurious dark hair and rubbed her cheeks with her hand, brushing away the greasepaint that gave her a Caucasian appearance. Beneath that makeup, her skin was a light brown, smooth with young womanhood, and as a false nose came off, the green eyes took a more lustrous tone. The classical features of a most beautiful Indian maid appeared before us. And Kritchna, eyes boggling, cried:

"Ashanti! Ashanti!"

"Hello, brother," the former Miss Underwood said, pointing her pistol at him.

It was impossible, I thought. Darshan's sister! Still alive!

"By the gods, Ashanti! We thought you were dead! Mother was heart-broken! I searched and searched, but—" He seemed to become aware there was a weapon in her hand. "What are you doing?"

The girl almost seemed sad. "What I must, Darshan. For you, I'm sorry, I truly am. But I'm not sorry he's gone..."—she gestured to the body on the floor—"or that he's going to go." She motioned to Sir Henry. "Or about the rest of these."

Slowly a light was beginning to dawn in my mind. "That's why you ran away as Rosemary Underwood! You weren't afraid the Sâr would recognize you—you were afraid Darshan would!" Tight-lipped, the girl nodded.

"For God's sake, why?" her brother asked.

She looked pointedly toward him. "Two reasons. First, revenge. You know what that bastard did to me. It wasn't enough he seduced me; he had to throw me out when I got pregnant. And he felt nothing when I lost the child. But then—then I met Peter." She smiled at her companion. "Unlike everyone else, he treated me kindly. He gave me money when I needed it. And we fell in love."

"But—but that's impossible!" Sir Henry interposed. "Peter, you're—"

"No, Father. I'm not. You assumed I was. Because I wouldn't sleep with the whores you and Alexander brought, even while you were married to Mother. It simply became easier to let you believe it. Even when you tried to marry me off to poor, foolish Christina here. Yes, my dear, I regret to say I had another lover while we were 'courting.' She had something I wanted; I had something she wanted. Love was just an added bonus to our relationship."

A cold smile crossed Ashanti's beautiful lips. "Which brings me to my second reason. You know how Father denied us our birthright, Darshan—the powers that were supposed to be ours. You didn't care. But I did. I wanted to learn. And Father wasn't going to let me. But then Peter came up with the perfect solution."

"Might I guess?" asked the Sâr. "Young Westenra wanted revenge on his family for years of neglect. You wanted revenge on the same. So you made a deal. Peter would arrange for you to meet other fakirs who would teach you the use of your psychic abilities. In return, when the time was right, you would use those abilities to kill his hated family. He must have paid to send you here alongside him, where you set yourself up as Spiritualist Rosemary Underwood. When news of the conference arose, the two of you saw your perfect opportunity."

"Not quite," Peter said. "That was the séance. Destroying the conference was just a bit of opportunistic coincidence. Our original plan was to simply kill Alexander and let Father destroy himself mourning—but why not remove Father's reputation and career while we were at it? The legend of the Rutherford Werewolf was too perfect not to use. Of course, Ashanti had never tried to form a *tulpa* before. It needed testing. So two nights before the conference, we tried to summon one up as a test."

"The footsteps on the roof," I said. "The thing that killed Colleen."

"Yes. Killing the cat wasn't intentional, by the by, if it salves your feelings. She simply got in the way. But we found that, despite her power, Ashanti still didn't have the expertise to create a *tulpa* out of whole cloth. The first fell apart very quickly. As you found out, Dickson."

"The goo I discovered."

"Yes. The remains of our first *tulpa* melting away."

"Still, we needed a solution, and quickly," Ashanti continued. "So we came up with the idea—we couldn't create a full *tulpa*, but we could create the shell of one. And if we put it over a living being—"

"You could temporarily control that being through your personified rage at the Westenras," the Sâr finished. "The person—Christina—would have no conscious control over her actions. The *tulpa*'s rage would be her driving force. A rage bent right toward the Westenras."

"But my mother—!" screamed Christina.

"Ah, yes. Poor Althea. We underestimated the bloodlust of the *tulpa* shell. But then, according to legend, the werewolf always kills first what it most loves." Peter shrugged. "But then, we all knew she'd been yearning to join her husband for ages, didn't we?"

Roxton cursed them, deeply and bitterly.

During this time, Sir Henry was sinking further and further to the floor, mopping his brow, unable to comprehend everything he was hearing. "This is not possible…"

"Oh, believe it, Father. Trust me; it's the last thing you ever will believe."

"So I suppose you intend to kill us all now?" The Sar raised an eyebrow. "I wonder how you intend to do so—if you shoot us, of course, the Police will certainly look to the only surviving Westenra."

"Naturally," Peter said, lowering the pistol. "But we don't need bullets to kill you." He smiled; a long, wide thing that seemed to split his face in two. As he did, for some reason Ashanti had closed her eyes. My first instinct was to charge them, but I knew they could fire within a second's notice.

"We'll bury the body of Alexander where no one will ever find it," Peter was continuing, and, somehow, he seemed to be becoming larger as he spoke. The hair on his arms was thickening, and a peculiar shimmering filled the air about him. His nose and lips seemed to be extending, pushing themselves out into one snout-like appendage. But no—it wasn't. Something from the air itself was surrounding the man, shaping itself like clay about the form of Peter Westenra, taking on fleshly color and solidity, then rippling as a thick mass of fur ran over it. The voice became deeper and harsher, the words more difficult to enunciate or understand. "But, you—what remains of you will be found." The hands seemed to extend out, fingers merging into a thick thumb and two digits. Claws appeared on the ends of them. "They'll never be able to put any of you back together, of course." The body slouched over as the knees of his legs seemingly reversed themselves, bending in the back like the hind legs of a dog. "And don't think your precious prayers or magic stones will work this time—they didn't work the first!"

Peter Westenra, now covered in the form of a Werewolf, threw back his head and howled.

Ashanti laughed and stepped aside, gazing admiringly at her handiwork. Unable to reach his rifle, Roxton placed himself before the women and poised himself. He knew he had no chance against this monster, but he was prepared to defend his niece till his last breath.

The rest of us, consciously or not, did the same. Save Sir Henry, who, terrified, shrank back, making little noises, making insane whimperings and a terrible smell emitting from between his legs.

Grinning and gurgling its terrible laugh, the Beast slowly rotated its neck across us, trying to decide whom it should kill first. Moving to the side, Ashanti's foot brushed against the outer rods of the Electric Pentacle. It made a dull clinking sound as she did, and the Beast, attention suddenly pricked, turned to see what had caused it. The red eyes fell upon the girl, who was stepping away from the contraption with a frown. As its gaze fell upon her, a stray thought flowed hysterically through my mind.

The werewolf always kills first what it most loves.

That must have been the reason. Whatever true feeling Peter Westenra may have had for Ashanti Kritchna, whatever humanity hadn't been dried up by years of being raised by Sir Henry, had been buried under the rage of the *tulpa*.

Ashanti clearly hadn't expected it. She looked up, surprised as the Beast turned fully toward her. "Peter?" Then she screamed as it leaped toward her.

"Kritchna! Dickson!" the Doctor yelled and all three of us dashed forward.

Roxton lunged for his rifle on the floor. Our only thoughts were to get this monster away from the girl and into the borders of the Pentacle. But it was too late for Ashanti. The great claws had reached out and ripped the flesh from her face, and she joined Alexander on the floor, dead instantly.

Kritchna roared and shoved the Beast forward. Startled, it tottered backward, stepping over the metal rods until it was in the center of the Pentacle.

"Appleby! Pray!" cried the Sâr and he began to dash about the Pentacle's edges, chanting in a loud voice. From various pockets, he brought forth Star-Stones, dropping them in what seemed to be random places (but weren't) and never pausing for a breath.

The *tulpa* paused, snarled, tried to step out of the Pentacle—but couldn't. Something seemed to be keeping it inside. It drew back, glaring at us evilly with its little red eyes

The Sâr paused long enough to cry, "Peter! Let it go! Let the *tulpa* dissolve! Otherwise, it will burn!"

He only got a howl in response and the Beast threw itself at the edge again and again. But it still failed to step beyond.

"Appleby! Keep praying!"

The butler did. As did the Sâr, continuing his monologue. And now the Beast was stepping back, wincing, just like I had seen in the garden of Westenra House. But now something new was happening.

All over the *tulpa*'s body, arms and legs and face, the fur and skin were bubbling

Tiny bursts of ectoplasm, like miniature geysers, were erupting from all parts of its torso and up and down its limbs, expending themselves in obscene, squishy pop-pop-pop noises that made me think of great boils somehow lancing themselves.

It turned to face us, painfully. It tottered uneasily on the bent, twisted appendages that served it for legs, as the true, human limbs of Peter Westenra beneath trembled uncontrollably. The look of pain on the monster's face was horrific. I could only guess what was happening to the man beneath. Peter Westenra was now controlled by the rage and hatred of his own creation, and lunged again and again at us. But for some reason it could not go beyond the last rod of the Electric Pentacle.

Behind me, I could hear Appleby increase the determination of his prayers; I could see before me the creature flinch with every word. For his part, the Sâr was practically dancing about the Pentacle, dropping Star-Stones and chanting his deep, unintelligible syllables. I sensed Gianetti and Christina clutching each other; I heard Lord John bravely but fumblingly load more bullets. But the *tulpa* would not relent.

It advanced, menacingly, but was forced to stop at the edge of the Pentacle. Placing its hand-paw against the air, it seemed to push against it, like an invisible wall was holding it back. The bubbling was continuing, and the top half of the Beast's head had almost melted away. I could see the beginnings of Peter's forehead show from beneath the ectoplasm. It was smoking—turning red and blistered as the power of the Pentacle and the incantations worked upon it, the fur on his arms peeling away to show black and burned human flesh, white bone beginning to show beneath the skin.

The fair hair had been burned away, leaving scorched scalp. Our nostrils were assailed with the stench of cooking meat. I myself could only stand there, watching in helpless fascination as everything I'd never believed in stood there and melted like it was made of hot treacle.

Craning its percolating neck, the *tulpa*'s eyes bored on the figure of the Doctor. It breathed heavily, as if gathering up its strength for one last attack. The latter had stopped both his dancing and chanting now, gazing evenly but with pity at the snarling Beast in the Pentacle. "It's over, Westenra. Surrender. You'll die if you do not. And I have no wish for that."

The creature that had been Peter Westenra snarled. And then, it leaped at the edge of the Pentacle with all its remaining might, shoving against the invisible "wall."

For a moment, I almost imagined the air bending outward like a bubble beneath its power. Then the bubble burst and the *tulpa* was outside the Pentacle. It seized the Sâr and knocked him to the carpet.

The werewolf form had almost entirely melted away by now, leaving a charred, burning, but still-alive Peter Westenra behind. But whatever humanity he had, if he indeed had ever truly had any, had been burned away as well. Only the beast remained. Teeth gleamed between the charcoal-black lips, reaching down for the Sâr's unprotected neck...

Instinctively, I lunged for the Beast. I heard something explode and then nothing but red pain was before my eyes as something tore into my side. Lord John had reacted automatically as well, shooting toward the Beast. But I had gotten in the way. I fell as the bullets tore into my hip.

All I repeat of what happened next, I cannot state with certainty absolutely happened. With a ball in my side and a ripped rag from Darshan's sleeve to staunch the blood, everything swam before my eyes as if from some opium dream. I was only vaguely aware that Kritchna was pulling me across the floor away from the fray. Lord John, his gun empty, yet pressed to the attack, slamming into the monster with the rifle butt as a club. Given the briefest of respites, the Sâr tried to reach out for a star-stone. But Peter stepped upon his hand. In one arm, with the strength of a madman, he held back Roxton, pushing the rifle away with the other. Then, with a heave he sent the aristocrat to the ground. Before he could rise, Westenra threw himself upon the Sâr, pushing back the Doctor's head to bare the tender flesh of the throat.

Peter threw back his head and howled.

Then screamed.

For he had forgotten the others.

On either side, two Star-Stones were suddenly and firmly pressed into his cheeks. Smoke poured from the indentations. But Darshan Kritchna and Christina Rutherford stood firm, shoving the stones further into his flesh; pressing harder and harder into its scorching folds.

Free, the Sâr began his chanting again—as did Appleby, who was now going through the only thing he could recall in his panic, the 23rd Psalm: "The Lord is my Shepherd; I shall not want.." I could hear the voice of Gianetti call out, a Latin prayer I could not immediately identify. And, lastly, despite my pain, I heard another voice ring out again and again, and could not believe it was my own:

"When the impossible has been eliminated, whatever remains, however improbable, must be the truth…When the impossible has been eliminated, whatever remains, however improbable, must be the truth—"

Peter Westenra, black and bleeding, trembled.

"Get back!" There was the click of a gun being primed, and then explosion. What remained of Peter's head went up in a ball of crimson fluid. The body twitched just one last, brief moment and became still.

Lord John staggered back, dropping his rifle.

There was only the sound of Sir Henry, sobbing in the background.

Somehow, in the midst of it all, I managed to roll over onto my back. I stared up at the beautiful face of Miss Gianetti, now hovering concernedly over me.

"You know, I was going to call in my mentor to see what he could make of all this," I said weakly. "But now, I believe I shall refrain."

"You're a very lucky young man, Dickson," the Sâr said as he finally finished wrapping the bandages around my waist. "You were in just the right position for the bullets to miss any organs. I wouldn't try anything strenuous for some time, but you should recover." He smiled broadly. "Certainly you shouldn't go hunting any more werewolves."

"Werewolves," I sighed, shaking my head wearily. "*Tulpas*. The occult."

"Even now you still do not believe, do you, Dickson? Not really."

I was quiet for a long time. Then: "It goes against everything I was ever taught, by my mentor or otherwise. Even now, I have to wonder if it could not have been some form of mass hypnosis, something we saw because we were supposed to see it."

The Doctor turned on the sink to wash his hands. "I cannot make you believe, Dickson," he said. "Only point you in the direction. If you choose to feel there's a rational explanation for all that has happened, I'm certain you'll come up with one. Until then, make your own decision." He tossed the towel aside. "Or perhaps you could try Appleby's way, and simply have a little faith."

The door opened and Lord John strolled in. "Well, I just got off the telephone with the Government. M's sending a contingent to wrap things up. You know M, don't you, Dickson?"

"We've met," I smiled.

"Well, he's asked that we all remain until his men get here. Wretched debriefings. God knows how they'll square all this with France, being as one of their most influential diplomats is dead, but they'll have to. He also said he'll take care of things with your employer, Dickson."

"Oh. Delightful." I could just see that. As well as the red ears I would get when I returned.

"By the way, I poured through Roger's old journals. Found a picture of the original 'werewolf.' Look." He held up a book, opening to a certain page. On it was a rough drawing; that of a spotted, sloped creature vaguely likes a dog, but much bigger and ratty. "A spotted hyena, just as we suspected. I've seen hundreds of them in Africa. Your theory must have been correct, Doctor— probably an exotic beast that originally escaped from some gipsy camp or other. There was never a *real* Werewolf of Rutherford Grange after all."

"Excellent," the Sâr declared as he picked up his omnipresent carpetbag. "But I'm afraid you'll have to give our regards to M. Miss Annunciata and I are leaving for Paris immediately."

"But—you can't go now! Not when M wants to speak with you!"

"Certainly I can. I despise debriefings. I'm sure you'll do fine without us." He paused at the door, turned back, and smiled. "Besides, knowing you, Dickson— you'll come up with *some* rational explanation for our departure."

Thus ended the Adventure of the Werewolf of Rutherford Grange. A cover story was set up about a huge and feral dog on the loose, killing people, but most seemed to accept it. It was better than the truth. Only a few more things remain to be said

Two days later, the funeral for Althea Rutherford was held. Sir Henry Westenra did not attend. He was a broken man: deprived of one son, betrayed by another, forever lost to both; his career was in ruins and no amount of favors owed could help him now. Eight months later, the town Constable found him with a broken neck and eyes rolled back to his forehead—he had taken a rope and hung himself from the very bridge his ancestor had hung three innocent people almost 300 years earlier. I wish I could say I felt sorry for him.

I presume the family of the Duc d'Origny had their own ceremony, but I was not privy to that. If the Sâr Dubnotal attended, I am not aware of it.

And, although I had sworn never to do so, almost a year to the day later I found myself in Wolfsbridge again, when I served as best man to a young Indian named Darshan Kritchna as Lord John Roxton gave Christina Rutherford away to be his wife. As I understand, most of her neighbors were more perturbed about Christina marrying out of her race than the fact her mother had been horribly killed, but I personally was delighted. The two had suffered much, and, in looking for comfort, found each other.

Darshan never told me what he did with his sister's body, and I did not ask. The vengeance he had wasted years trying to gain had been ripped from him and it was painful for him to face it. In the end, they decided to return to India, where I understand Roxton used his contacts to gain obtain Darshan a comfortable position with the Government. Christina settled down to a contented motherhood. Over the years I have since lost contact with the two, but if they should ever happen to read this manuscript, I would have them know I continue to wish them both the best.

Appleby left Service, even at his age, to finally fulfill his dream of becoming a minister. As you might have heard, eventually he gained quite a reputation for himself as a lecturer—*against* the ilk of Spiritualism and the occult. Once, several years later, I had occasion to meet him unexpectedly on a London street and inquire about his new-found calling. In reply, it was clear he still respected the memory of the Sâr but told me, "A fake séance raised a *tulpa*, Mr. Dickson. Have you any idea what an *actual* one might call up?"

I had no answer to that.

As for myself, I returned to my apprenticeship with Mr. Blake, where my ears were promptly blistered for not calling him in immediately. Then he listened in fascination while I told him what happened. I returned to school and eventually did realize my dream of opening my own agency—although it took the Great War and much Intelligence work to finally work a callow youth into a mature, fully reasoning adult. You may have read some exaggerated versions of my adventures in the popular magazines.

Yet to this day, I still don't know what to think about the "Werewolf of Rutherford Grange." So, for the most part, I simply ignore the memory. A mind so powerful it can call entities into being right out of the aether? A mixture of science and the supernatural to call up the ghosts of the dead? It still goes against everything I have ever held sacred being perfectly aware all the while, of course, of the unique irony in a Skeptic holding anything at all to be "sacred.").

What's that, you say? And whatever happened to Gianetti and the Sâr Dubnotal?

In truth, I am glad I am unable to tell you. For I fully intend never to have a second encounter with them, as long as I can help it!

Beware the Beasts

Planet Soror, the Future

It really was a lovely afternoon for tea. The brief summer shower had passed, filling the air with the pleasant tang of wet earth and grass. In the garden behind Jinn's villa, songbirds twittered from tree to tree, while a red squirrel, looking for nuts, paused inquisitively upon a branch to gaze down at the strange party, then dash back into the leaves, tail twitching furiously.

"Another cup, perhaps?" Jinn asked his honored guest.

Doctor Omega leaned back in his chair and abstained, contentment practically pouring out of him.

"Oh, heavens, certainly not. I couldn't eat another bite."

"More jam, Tiziraou?"

Phyllis, Jinn's lovely wife, proffered a dish to the little creature sitting next to her.

"Thank you, please," the tiny, macroencephalic Martian chirped in its high-pitched voice, pushing its plate forward, perhaps more eagerly than necessary. Unable to chew most solid foods, the small alien was often forced to make do with more liquified sustenance. As a result, he had become practically addicted to the melange of sweet jams and jellies his planet had never produced, but that were so easily obtainable in far-off Normandy.

The Doctor tut-tutted, but otherwise said nothing. After nearly dying in his heroic attempt to help save this world, he figured that Tiziraou was entitled to a bit of gluttony.

At the edge of the pond, a swan-like creature dipped its long, elegant neck deep into the water, looking for food. Along all sides of the villa, Phyllis' beloved flowers were in full bloom, attracting the pleasant buzzing of honeybees.

"I still don't know how to thank you, Doctor," Jinn stated. "If not for you and Tiziraou, Soror would have ceased to exist, in the blink of an eye. How could we possibly repay you? We owe you everything."

"Oh, I wouldn't say 'everything,' my boy." The Doctor casually waved off the compliment, but his face was a blazing display of self-satisfaction. "I'm hardly responsible. Indeed, we wouldn't even have known of the whole affair if we hadn't encountered that lost spaceman during our travels, would we, Tiziraou? Too bad he refuses to leave my *Cosmos* to join us, but I'm not going to force him."

Steepling his fingers together, he gazed into the sky and harrumphed. "The mere effrontery of it all. This Q creature... Deciding he doesn't like the way a planet is shaping up, so he takes it upon himself to create a variant, to change things to see if he likes it better another way... Still, we certainly placed a spanner into his works, didn't we, hmm? Perhaps he'll think twice next time before playing with the timelines again."

"I certainly hope so, Doctor," said Jinn.

"You know what you have to do now, hmm?" said Doctor Omega, looking at them sternly.

Phyllis put in quietly. "I still cannot get over the notion..."

"I know what you're going to say, my dear. But you have no choice."

"Do we?" Jinn's voice was raised in protest, but he refused to raise his eyes to meet the Doctor's. "What can we do? We're merely two people. Yet you ask us to alter hundreds of years of hatred and..."

"Entire worlds have turned on the actions of just one person, Jinn. Believe me. I know. And it has to begin somewhere."

"But—but you don't understand!" Phyllis cried. "From our very childhood, we are taught to hate and fear the beasts. Of all creatures, only they hunt and kill for the sheer pleasure of it; only they slaughter for the sake of slaughter. Even their own kind, they kill. The beasts are *monsters*, Doctor. How can you ask us to put all that aside?"

"Because you must, child. Because for all the just, equitable society you have tried to create here on Soror, it still amounts to nothing if even one sentient creature cannot participate in it. You say the beasts are monsters? You're right; they are. I know that better than anyone. They're killers. Murderers. But they are also so much more." Once again, he glanced to the sky, as if gathering his thoughts. "I have seen the destinies of countless races throughout this universe, my friends. I have seen entire civilizations born, grow and die, either slowly or quickly, all too often by their own hands. But rarely have I seen one with so much potential, so much ability to turn their ways to either good or evil. It would be a crime against the universe if you did not allow them that chance." Pushing his cup aside, he leaned forward expectantly. "And remember, to them, *you* are the beasts. You are the ones who hunt them without cause; who seem to hate them for the mere sake of hating them."

Doctor Omega pointed a finger up to the alien sun above. "Finally, also remember that your planet originally had no existence. You're a slice of time brought into existence by Q. Your civilization, for all its greatness and wonder, exists only because of a whim. Once his experiment was done, he would have destroyed you, if we hadn't happened along... You say you owe me? Then repay me by letting the beasts into your society. It can be done. If you want to."

Slowly, Jinn and Phyllis looked at each other. Then, slowly, they bowed their heads in acceptance.

"Good," said the Doctor, smiling. "I knew you'd agree. As I said, you are a just society. You, too, deserve to be part of the universe. And I'm certain you'll make it."

Reaching into his frock coat, he pulled a large gold watch. "Time we got back to the *Cosmos*, eh, Tiziraou? We've still got to get that astronaut back to his own time and space. Come along!"

He stood, then wagged one finger warningly. "If you ever doubt the rightness of letting the beasts into your society," he said, "think on how they treat your own people on their world."

Gravely, he shook hands with his hosts. Tiziraou bowed comically. Then, with a promise to return one day, the two travelers sauntered off deeper into the garden, where they had left their ship.

Phyllis settled in next to her beloved Jinn.

"Could it be true, darling?" she asked. "Could we really civilize those creatures and let them into our society as equals?"

Frowning, the chimpanzee shook his head. "I don't know, my love. Man is such a peculiar beast..."

Tros Must Be Crazy!

Gaul, 55 B.C.

The warrior had to admit he felt nervous, although he'd never say as much to his crew. It was hard enough keeping them in line on ordinary days. Let alone on a night like this...

The late autumn wind was chill, and the warrior quietly drew his cloak tighter. Above, the Moon took on a pale, leprous tinge. He was but a rank initiate into the Mysteries, but even he could deduce bad omens when he saw them.

Perhaps this was not one of my best ideas....but to defeat Caesar, I would ally myself with anyone, yea, even with the damned, twisted Wyrms of the Earth themselves! he thought.

The tiny landing craft drew up against the shore and two of his swarthy, battered crew stumbled out to pull it ashore, both reeking of stale ale and fresh urine. It was a wonder they had even gotten the craft this far without sinking it. Ignoring them, the warrior climbed out before they had finished and waded the last few feet to shore, carefully examining the surroundings as was his wont. The beach, silent and empty, stretched along for miles without obstruction. At its edge, it sloped slowly upward, its sandy waste vanishing into the midst of black, fertile forest. A few night birds cried out.

Gesturing to his men to wait, the warrior moved forward boldly across the beach, up the slope and to the very border of the thick, seemingly impenetrable trees.

"You may as well come out," he called, calmly but commandingly. "I know you are there."

For a moment, the only answer was silence. Then, the vegetation was brushed away, and slowly from the foliage stepped a bent, wizened figure, long-bearded, with every joint creaking.

The warrior grimaced in spite of himself. As a novice, he should bow before the Druid with respect, but great age had rendered the man so unattractive it was difficult to pay him proper homage. The figure grinned, showing a crooked mouth of yellow teeth, and pulled his crimson cloak closer to ward off the cold.

"You are far from Samothrace, my friend."

"That matters little. What does is whether you have what we agreed upon, Druid. Do you?"

Chuckling a bubbly, acidic laugh, the Druid reached a scrawny arm into his cloak. "I do. But what about you?"

The warrior dared turn his head enough to nod toward his men. At his signal, two reached down into the boat and then approached, lugging between them a huge chest. They dropped it at their leader's feet and backtracked, gazing apprehensively upon the white-haired Druid.

The warrior opened the chest.

"There," he said. "The treasure of the Picts. It was simple enough to take it. Over the centuries, they have descended into grotesque parodies of their former selves. Only in their aristocracy do they retain their old blood..."

The warrior's mouth twisted a moment, recalling the mighty battle he had had with their king. Surely, that man could have been a great thorn in Caesar's side. That, or his son, or his son's son... Enough. Time to get what he came for.

"I have given you what you desired, Druid. And now, it is your turn."

The ancient Druid's ugly smile drew wider. "As you wish." His arm withdrew from the cloak and a taloned, liver-spotted hand held forth a small vial. "Here. Drink this and all your troubles with Caesar will be over."

With skeptical fingers, the warrior's hand closed over the vial. He could hear a strange potion sloshing about within. "And just how do I know this sorcery you brag about so well shall truly work?"

"Do you truly doubt my—"

The admonishment was never completed. From behind the brush, a great scream was heard and, suddenly, the warrior witnessed the sight of a man, clad in Roman armor and helmet, shooting up over the trees in a wide arc, passing over the beach a good 20 feet in the air and coming to a hard splash not half a mile from shore. For a moment the calm sea foamed, then settled. The Roman soldier was gone.

"Oops! Sorry!" From the forest, a head, bearing a huge nose and scraggly yellow mustache that seemed even huger, popped out. From the warrior's viewpoint, the person owning them must have been smaller than even a Pict. "Just a spy I had to take care of! Sorry to interrupt!" It popped back into the foliage.

The white-cloaked Druid gave the warrior a sardonic look.

He sighed. "I'll take 20."

Who Made Me Such A Woman?

Tokyo, November 1945

At long last, the storm had finally ended. But Kano-to Yoshimuta felt no cleansing from the rain.

The remaining precipitation felt cold and dirty; a soggy premonition of colder, grayer days to come. Grimacing, Kanoto drew the nape of her cloak closer. It was a raggedy, threadbare thing; patched in far too many places; yet, for a body that had not, all that long ago, known the finest European fashions money could buy, it at least kept one warm. Unfortunately the cheap straw hat pulled low down her brow was a much poorer thing; sending thick, dribbly rivulets drenching down upon her feet. Mind you, becoming soaked would have been inescapable, for she could take not even one step which did not result in at least one foot being immersed in the filthy concrete ponds pitting what had once been one of the city's side thoroughfares.

The Yankees, they said, were pouring millions of dollars into the economy to help facilitate Tokyo's rebuilding, but any coinage the *gai-jin* may be granting their newest protectorate out of the goodness of their newly-victorious heart had yet to even begin to penetrate here. The Yurakucho District didn't have enough sniveling jackals milling about MacArthur and his cronies to convince them to help out yet. Everywhere rested the

162

remains of fire-bombings past: the abandoned, rusting skeletons of charcoal-powered cars; crumbling piles of stone and masonry; the blackened, ashy edges outlining what had once been paper-walled homes and businesses. And then, there were the residents, crawling about the wreckage. Draped low in one of the abandoned autos seats, a sallow, sickly man in the filthy remains of an Imperial Navy uniform lay snoring, an empty bottle of beer bought from some American clutched to his chest. Two old biddies pushed past, bent and crone-like, mumbling to themselves that, hopefully, the Black Market might have some meat today. And, crouched next to the flowing gutter, an urchin, perhaps all of eight years old, suddenly jerked his hand down into the brown water to bring up the dregs of a used cigarette, not even worth being called a butt, and dragged on it with all his strength.

Dogs, she thought. *Cowed beaten dogs whimpering at the feet of their masters.*

THESE were the loyal Sons and Daughters of the Emperor; the proud scions of samurai and ronin, who, only a few years ago, had pledged to their gods and ancestors they would willingly take their own lives and the lives of their children rather than submit to the command of white, barbarian *gai-jin.*

Pathetic. Absolutely pathetic.

Crawling around in garbage like common rats. And yet, she knew, whatever was happening here was nothing compared to the suffering she had just left in Nagasaki.

Nagasaki. Her home. Her family.

Even though once she would have died rather than acknowledge their existence, the relatives who had taken her in told her the gods must have chosen to save her, smiling sadly, as if their feeble attempts at empathy could even begin to comfort her. Surely the Gods of Nippon had spared her for her great intelligence, they said; surely they must have some great plan for her future. Perhaps to invent something that would finally end this world's mad continual rush to war and ruin, in memory of her husband and children. They would have wanted that, they said. For her to go on and create something Great and Good out of such world-wide devastation.

They knew nothing. About her family or about her. Besides, there was only one god Kanoto Yoshimuta believed in anymore.

The God of Vengeance.

The rain had muted to a dull drizzle. Kanoto kept on walking. For some, the exercise would have been a way to dull stress. For her, it was a way to keep her rage kindled; to keep the raging fire lit within her soul. The people had failed Nippon. The military had failed Nippon. The gods-damned EMPEROR had failed Nippon. But she would not. No. If she lived to be a hundred, a thousand, a million, two names would remain forever etched into her brain.

Hiroshima.

Nagasaki.

Always and forever, until America burned like they did.

A series of odd sounds, almost animal-like, brought her out of her reverie. She was seemingly alone now, in a small alley between a few surviving buildings. In the gloom, about a hundred yards ahead, a long, irregular piece of sheet metal had been propped up at an angle alongside one of the alley walls. The sounds came from there.

After a moment, the low, moaning grunting stopped. Two figures emerged from the makeshift shelter. The first was the mere slip of a girl, pockmarked and plain, perhaps sixteen or so. Turning, she held her hand out, palm upward, toward her companion.

Kanoto's eyes narrowed. *"Panpan,"* she breathed. A common prostitute.

Then she thought, no, not just a *common* trollop. For the man who had emerged with her was no son of Nippon. Tall and blond, pink-faced and smirking, clad in the uniform of an American soldier, he was just buckling up his belt as he came out.

The girl was a traitor. Making it her business to "assist" the invaders looking for comfort from their misfortune in being so, so far from home.

They apparently had not seen her. Kanoto watched as the G.I., looking very self-satisfied, put back on his jacket and clamped his hat down. He gazed down at the expectant hand, laughed, and commented, in English, "You gotta be kiddin' me. It was OK, but nothin' to write home about. I've had twice as good in the Philippines."

The look upon her face showed the child might not have understood the words but received the meaning clearly enough. "Sonofbitch! Bastard!" she squawked in cracked, infuriated English. "Gimme money!" She reached out as if to grab him.

With a swift backhand he slapped her to the ground. "Little Jap cunt," he growled. "You should feel honored that a real American even thought about doing you. God knows, we should have wiped out the lot of you when we had the chance—Hey!"

The interjection was because Kanoto had done two things. First, almost idly she had reached into her cloak, fiddling within it for a moment. Then, she had taken it back out and approached the soldier while he was giving his harangue. She gently tapped the man upon the shoulder with her other hand. Unthinkingly, he turned.

—And Kanoto raked the nails of her other hand right across his throat.

They dug deep into the flesh of the G.I.'s neck. He staggered back, clutching at the red daubs of blood spotting under his chin.

"You little—!" he began, but never finished. For suddenly the soldier's eyes glazed, rolling up like they were trying to gaze upon his scalp. Then, he toppled forward, a sawed tree in an American uniform, down unmoving into the muck.

He was quite dead.

Kanoto rolled the body over with her foot. "The first. You are only the first." Then she turned to the *pan-pan*.

The girl, her eyes wide, was finally beginning to pull herself back up. A well-aimed kick in the backside sent her down again. "You *fool*," Kanoto hissed down at the struggling girl. "You miserable little *fool!*" She reached down to jerk the girl over, forcing her to look up at her. Quite intentionally, she was using the other hand, the one that had not touched the G.I., to do so. "How could you? How could you sell your country and your race just to pleasure *them*? Who made you such a woman?"

The girl tried to speak and gagged, puking up the ground-filth she had swallowed. "Do you think I want to?" she choked out at last. "My family is dead! I have no job and no money to buy food! I'm hungry!"

"Hungry?" She slapped the little whore's face. "*Hungry?* You don't think *I'm* not hungry? But do you

166

see me disrobing for the enemy simply to fill my belly? Our sacred ancestors would have starved before humiliating themselves in such a way! But you—you're like all the cowards in this land who would rather bow the knee to barbarians rather than fight them to the last breath! You shame our ancestors and you shame our race! Did Hiroshima, Nagasaki mean nothing to you? I should—" Slowly she drew back her other hand.

"Really, Kanoto."

The interrupting voice was quiet, inoffensive. As was the figure she saw when she turned. Somehow, the limousine had arrived in the alley behind her absolutely silently. The little man stood regarding her calmly, in that clinical way he had that reminded her of the way she looked at lab animals. Disinterestedly, but without contempt. That would have been a waste of emotion.

"You."

He smiled, a glint of gold-capped teeth showing. His Prussian hairstyle and immaculate Western suit was well-protected by the shield of a giant umbrella. Beside him, arms folded, stood a uniformed driver, faceless and mute, looking as though the only thoughts that ever entered his head were the ones his companion gave him.

The little man shook his head, gazing down at the body of the former American. "Oh, Kanoto. Death is always a tragedy, is it not?" He sighed. "Well, I suppose we cannot just leave the poor fellow lying there on the ground." He turned to the driver. "Do see if you can find a better place for him. One where he can lie in peace and quiet for a while. A considerable while."

Wordlessly, the driver stepped forward and, with effortless ease, lifted the body. His anonymous face appeared neither perturbed nor pleased by his assignment. In a moment, he had vanished from Kanoto's sight, lugging his burden with him. His master, meanwhile, had returned his attention to the ladies.

"Kindly lower your hand and release that poor girl, Kanoto," he purred calmly. "Poison under the nails? That's a bit beneath you, even when dealing with an American." He smiled kindly upon the girl. Then from a pocket he proffered a thick wad of green bills.

The *panpan's* eyes goggled. "American dollars!"

"Indeed. Go. Buy yourself food. With one caveat— you're going to conveniently forget everything you have seen here today, yes? You shall? Oh, that is so very nice. Here, my dear." The girl had just enough time to seize the wad with a pair of grubby hands before she was darting out of the alley.

Kanoto glared at him bitterly. "You should not have let her go."

He sighed again. "Kanoto, Kanoto, Kanoto. There are more pressing problems in Nippon today than a girl who has to spread her legs for her supper. I see you have not changed. Well—perhaps you have." He regarded her solemnly; the hard creases in her face; the gray prematurely slicing through her hair. "The years have not been kind to you, I fear, my dear. Once your beauty was legend from Kyoto to Sapporo."

Her eyes glittered with dagger points. "Not to mention Nagasaki. And Hiroshima. The War has been hard on all of us, old friend."

"Ah, too true, too true," her companion bowed. "I, too, have suffered loss in this War."

"Have you, now?" Kanoto replied sardonically. She glanced toward the limo. "You seem to be navigating the shortages of Tokyo quite well, in my opinion."

"Ah. Do not let my apparent outward prosperity fool you, my dear. I—"

"What do you want?"

" 'Want,' Kanoto? Why should I 'want' anything? Can't two old friends simply meet by coincidence upon the street and reminisce of old times?"

"You do not 'do' coincidence. You never have. I ask again—what do you *want?*"

He sighed once more; this one deepest of all. "Let us go for a drive and relieve ourselves of this inclement weather, Kanoto," he said, opening the limo door. The driver had returned from wherever it was he had stashed the corpse. "Please, do have a seat."

Warily, Kanoto slipped beside him into the limo. When she sat, she practically sank into the leather-covered seat. Her companion moved in besides her. "Just around the block for now, please," he ordered through a speaking tube. With an imperceptible purr of engines, the limo began to move.

"May I offer you a drink to ward the weather's chill away?" he gestured toward the built-in bar. "I have champagne and brandy; and here is a very fine Chianti. No? Well, I believe I shall have some of this Dom Perignon '23. Very difficult to come by these days, as you might guess."

Kanoto remained silent.

He paused, sipping the wine, seemingly in some thought. "I was very sorry to hear about your husband, Kanoto," he said at last. "Despite our differences, I counted him as a true friend."

She shuffled, uncomfortably it seemed. "As he did you," she admitted at last. "Although he could never understand what it was you truly wanted for Nippon."

"I wanted—and still want—just as he did. The cultural and economic dominance of our country over the world. We merely disagreed about method. I have always argued that we should have acted slowly and gradually to spread our ways; to let the *gai-jin* see the superiority of our culture and *want* to become a part of it, rather than be forced to. Your husband preferred...a faster method."

She frowned. "And should he have not?" she demanded. "We were surrounded! Once, we were happy enough to ignore the outside world and simply stay on our island. But, no, the Americans couldn't have that. They had to 'open' us up to the world—a world that treated us as, as some sort of second-class creature because of the shape of our eyes and the color of our skin! It wasn't enough they had to force us to buy their junk and scrap—they had to wink and nod behind our backs while they did it!"

"So we went to war...and now they can wink and nod in our faces." He put aside his glass. "Hurrying got us quite far, did it not? No, do not make faces at me, my dear. War solved nothing for us. Now we must embrace the ways of Peace and see where that leads."

"With the destroyers of Nagasaki? Never!"

"Never?"

"Never! Why are you telling me this?"

He closed his eyes, and for the first time she saw a play of emotion upon his face. "I know, Kanoto."

And a deep chill fell through her. "K-know?" she stuttered. "Know what?"

"Everything."

"I—"

"Everything. Your letters to Ishii about 'how the war will continue.' Your correspondence with certain, ah, *disaffected* officers in our military. Your meetings with the Yakuza and what remains of the Black Dragon Society. I even know how you have been trying to bribe fishing boats to take you to that obscure little island to collect specimens of its most interesting fungi. Believe me, I have already warned General MacArthur not to be eating mushrooms anytime soon." He stared at her angrily. "Did you truly believe that I could not discover this, Kanoto? That I would not know?"

Kanoto Yoshimuta's face lowered, arced, twisted and squeezed; then straightened. "All right," she said. "So you know. So what now?"

"I would know why you are doing this."

"Why? Isn't it obvious?" she screamed; her voice ringing in the limited space. "I am doing it to rid the world of the conquerors of Nippon! I am doing it for the people of Hiroshima and Nagasaki! I am doing it—yes, I confess—for the deaths of my family! I am doing it for revenge!"

"For Nippon?" His face was impassive.

"Yes!"

"For your family?"

"Yes!" she howled.

"Are you certain?"

She stopped dead. "What do you mean?" she hissed through tight lips.

He leaned back into the seat and stayed quiet for a moment, tapping his fingers. Then: "My dear, do you know why we chose to send such agents to the United States as we did—Sakima and Haruchi and so forth?"

"Of course. They were loyal Sons of the Emperor, willing to lay down their lives for the Cause."

"Wrong," he replied softly. "We sent them because they were psychopaths."

He raised a hand. "No—do not protest. You know what they were as well as I. Together or separately, they had caused consternation in this country before the War.

And would have done so again—if they hadn't been, in their own way, patriotic. So when they volunteered in order to try to spill American blood for a change, we let them. If they completed their missions, well and good. If not…Nippon would not suffer greatly for their loss."

He reached into his jacket and removed a cigarette box. Calmly he tapped one out. "A smoke? Lucky Strikes, I believe they are called. I got them from an Australian with far too many tattoos. No? Well." He sucked in a deep draught of American tobacco. "Back to what I was saying. They were problems for us, Kanoto. Problems we had to get rid of. Indeed, at one time we had an entire list of 'problems' we intended to send overseas. I took you and your husband off that list."

Her eyes widened. "What? Are you telling me that—"

"Oh, yes." A whisp of smoke drifted lazily upward. "There are those of us who have regarded you and yours… *disquietly* for some time, my dear."

For once she had no idea what to say. "But…but…Everything I have ever done was for the glory and honor of Nippon! *Everything!*"

"And that is why you habitually carry poison around to place upon your fingernails? Answer me that, hmm? And there are other things—for example, that strange and mysterious city hidden deep in China, founded, of all things, by fleeing 18th century Protestants? They had mastered certain elements of light and sound unknown to the rest of the world, according to reports: secrets that could have been very useful to us in the War. Yet, for some reason, when you and your husband returned from the 1937 expedition, you reported that the city, and all its wonders, had been forcibly destroyed."

"We had to, you fool! Otherwise Doctor Natas…"

"…Would have seized it for himself? Perhaps. Or—you have always been quick to resent those somewhat more successful than yourself, my dear. Serizawa, for one. I seem to remember several letters in the science journals mocking his oxygen experiments. And it is no secret you had been having troubles with your own researches into light. Could it possibly be that you were so infuriated that a ragtag little city of inbred refugees—and *white* refugees at that—had mastered what you could not that you ordered the entire city destroyed in a fit of pique?"

"That—never—happened," she hissed through her teeth.

"Did it not? And just what line of research were you investigating when Hiroshima and Nagasaki occurred, hmm? You bragged you were going to be quite the 'madame of the atom,' as I recall. So tell me, my dear old friend—is your wrath truly because the American brought the Thunder down upon Nippon…or is it because they stole your own thunder?" Suddenly his cigarette was snapping in two. "When we were both young and walked hand-in-hand in the countryside, I would never have dreamed this of you. What happened to you, Kanoto? Who made you such a woman?"

She could not longer stop herself. With an animal snarl she lunged at him, driving her fingernails toward his throat. But he was faster. Suddenly her digits were being seized in an iron grip. Instantly, Kanoto drew back. As small and inoffensive as her companion appeared, she knew he could kill her in twelve different ways before she drew her next breath.

"Do not do that again." He clenched a bit tighter, enough so she could feel her bones creak. *"Ever."*

Slowly, very slowly, she lowered her arm, massaging the fingers. "My husband died in Hiroshima," she said simply. "My children died. Horribly. And you ask me to forgive the Americans for that?"

"As I said, you are not the only one to suffer from the war. I, too, lost much." For a brief instant she saw the look of pain skit across his features, then it was gone. "But the war is over. We lost. We would have lost even if the Americans hadn't dropped the bombs. And it would have cost us far, far more than we lost even on that terrible day."

She was silent.

He reached out to seize her hand again, but gently this time. A gentleness she had not felt from him for a very long time. "Our people are weary and hungry, my dear. They are sick of blood and death. It is time to take the energies of Nippon and parlay them in a new direction. Nippon can be as great as it was meant to be—but not as an Empire. Instead, we must be an Example. An example for the new post-war world that is coming. You could be at the forefront of that world, Kanoto. But you must give up this hatred and jealousy. I will not allow our country to become embroiled in another war it cannot afford to fight."

He picked up the tube and ordered the car to stop. Then he reached over and opened the door for her.

"Go, Kanoto. I give you two choices. Come forward with us and help make a true future for Nippon. Or continue to try to take your oh-so-precious vengeance upon the Americans. I shall not try to stop you if you do. But I will not aid you, either. And know this—if in your mad quest you do anything—*anything*—to bring the wrath of America down upon the people of Nippon again, I shall not rest until your head is perched upon a pike in my garden. And that would make me so very unhappy."

She pressed her lips tightly. "I would expect no less, old friend."

Then she climbed out of the limousine.

He slammed the door shut. Then, after a moment, the window rolled down and Mr. Moto gazed upon her for the last time. "Consider carefully, Kanoto. I have made my decision. Now it is time to make yours." The window closed and with its smooth purr the limo moved forward, across the littered street with its shattered corpses of buildings toward the Sun just beginning to peek from the clouds. Kanoto Yoshimuta watched it leave.

She kept her promise. She did think.

She thought about Nippon.

She thought about America.

She thought of the centuries of the samurai; the glory of a world won by blood and battle.

She thought about her husband and children, killed in an instant flash of atomic power; the only thing left to remind her of their existence photographic after-images on a brick wall.

She thought about her work, and how it might have save them all.

How the Americans…

Then, very deliberately, she turned her back and faced the retreating dark.

Peace is for fools and cowards, she thought, *not me. I am not that kind of woman.* She paused, and smiled ironically. *Who made me such a woman?*

I did. And I shall make myself such a woman as this world has never seen.

For Hiroshima.

For Nagasaki.

For myself and what they took from me. My family and my...

For my family.

Courtesy of the Madame of the Atom.

No. That sounds terrible.

Courtesy of Madame Atomos.

Sacrebleu!

It was child's play to break into the Louvre, despite its much-vaunted (and highly publicized) alarm systems.

Like a sleek black angel fallen from above, the dark-clad woman known as Irma Vep slipped across the rooftops, and paused before a skylight hidden within the ceiling of the famed museum. She heard the shrill wail of a police car raising a warning, but it was moving to the south. Irma Vep smiled drily. Rumor had it that some more of Moreau's vile concoctions were loose on the streets; she didn't know if this was true, but it provided a convenient distraction. Within seconds, she had disabled the skylight's security systems, opened the glass and, seconds later, she was ratcheting herself downward with a silk cord all the way to the floor below.

Silently, she smiled again, wondering what her old mentor might have thought. She had learned much from Arsène Lupin, before he discovered her true nature. That was the weakness Ganimard would never grasp: a beautiful face and supple body could lure even the most famous men into more traps than they would ever know.

The great museum was coldly silent in the darkness. Irma Vep refused to risk a light; she had already memorized every step she would need. She knew that the diamond was there. *The* diamond. The Pink Panther.

And she meant to have it.

The footfalls of a cat would have been less silent than the black-clad siren as she slipped down the hall.

Her eyes were already beginning to adjust to the inky blackness, and her every sense was pricked to the fullest. There was the slightest scent of a peculiarly acrid smell coming from somewhere, but it was very faint.

Probably harmless, she thought.

Then, slow, methodical footsteps rang out ploddingly ahead. Irma Vep swiftly ducked beneath a velvet rope separating a small construction area from the main lobby. She hugged tensely to the wall.

A guard. Just be careful, nothing to worry about.

Her slim, gloved hand dipped into a pouch slung across her hip, and tossed what appeared to be a small marble across the floor. The flash from the guard's lamp reflected against it, and she saw two feet cautiously, but curiously approach the sphere. Then the gas seeped out and the night watchman slumped helplessly to the ground.

That was easy enough. Irma Vep slipped back under the rope, pausing just long enough to glance back toward her hiding place. With the small, soft glow of the guard's discarded flashlight, she could just make out the placard: *WET PAINT*. Damn! Now the back of her body stocking probably had a nice line of white paint right down the center of it. Ah well. She could always get another. With the Pink Panther in hand, she could buy millions of…

Enough. Back to the steps. Thirty-one, thirty-two, thirty-three…

The wires and bells of the security system were laughable. A midnight cloud, Irma Vep slinked to the center of the room and stood for a moment, regarding her prize. Men had killed for the Pink Panther. And now the germ was hers—only hers.

Expertly, she began to cut through the glass case protecting the diamond. Her back felt damp and sticky, but that was small price to pay. Odd how that acrid smell seemed to becoming stronger—

—And that's when the giant skunk hit her!.

"Ahhhh, my darling, you have been waiting all ze life for someone such as I, no? Mmm mmm mmm! You may call me Pépé of ze Moulin Rouge, for I intend to be making ze beautiful music with you, mmm mmm mmm…"

A-A-A-Au Revoir, Folks!

"Professor Krausse" is one of the most interesting of Harry Dickson's adventures. It was initially published in No. 141 of the French edition, entitled L'Étoile à Sept Branches *[The Seven-Pointed Star]. The title story being too short, Jean Ray, then writer/editor/adapter of the series, added two extra stories, one called "Le Rituel de la Mort" [The Ritual of Death], a rather transparent swipe of Maurice Leblanc's "Sherlock Holmes Arrives Too Late" (included in our edition of* The Hollow Needle*). The other was "Professor Krausse," which lifts the veil on Dickson's activities right after the Great War...*

Professor Krausse

(*adapted by Jean-Marc & Randy Lofficier*)

Preamble

"In my long career, I have fought many strange and fearsome villains, commonly known as 'mad scientists,'" said Harry Dickson. "I crossed swords with Doctor Mysteras and Professor Drumm, and others whose names I've now forgotten, and no doubt I'll fight more in the future, but none were as singular as Professor Krausse. With him, we enter a realm of uncertainty worthy of the great E.T.A. Hoffman, in which finding one's way through the darkness is always difficult...

"My first encounter with the Professor took place in Berlin soon after the Armistice of November 1918. The Spartacist uprising had just been bloodily put down and the German capital was prey to nameless passions. Misery and debauchery were the twin heralds of the new regime.

"Men in uniforms begged openly in the streets; newly made widows, who had once belonged to the German aristocracy, were bartering their favors for a meal, a pint of beer, or, worse, a glass of gin. It was a tragic spectacle. As for myself, I was working for British intelligence and had just finished an inspection of the notorious Moabit prison, to check if the rumors that some of our secret agents were still being held there were true. As it turned out, that wasn't the case, so my visit was rather short.

"The hours I had spent in that dark and dismal place made me want fresh air, so I decided to stretch my legs and take a stroll through the neighborhood, even though it was a particularly miserable part of the city.

"As I was walking, I suddenly smelled a rather appetizing odor. Upon investigation, I found that it came from the dark end of a gloomy back alley. I still remember its name, which was embossed on an enameled plate: *Nachtrabengasse*, or Night Raven Street.

"It struck me as a rather gothic and melodramatic name, but my curiosity had been awakened and I wanted to learn more—plus, there was that mouth-watering smell…

"I soon discovered a tavern, the entrance of which opened at the top of a massive flight of stone steps. Its sign swung softly in the night air and read: *Zum Treppchen bei Rolff Froschmeier*. A blackboard advertised the day's specials: *Kalbs und Schweinebraten*, roasted veal and pork; *Spickgans, bratkartoffeln und Gemüse*, smoked goose, roasted potatoes and vegetables; *Wurstsalad*, sausage salad; *Delikatessen*, cold cuts;

Klobst, Obst und Kugel, fruits and pastries. After four years of rationing and *ersatz* foods, it was enough to make anyone salivate. So I went in.

"Inside, not unexpectedly, the tavern was quite full, and I had trouble finding a table. I ended up sitting next to a former Imperial Guardsman wearing a faded uniform. He was a charming fellow and he soon introduced me to the landlord, Herr Froschmeier, an awful, gnome-like man wearing a silly pink bonnet.

"Soon, I was served the evening's special: a plate of excellent vegetables with a slice of roasted pork *au jus*. I can't explain why, but I didn't touch the meat which was too pink and too slimy for my taste. My new acquaintance, however, had no problem eating it voraciously, with my blessings, after he had finished his own portion.

"The crowd was a mixed lot; I noticed there were many *schiebers*, war profiteers and black marketers. A lot of money was being spent freely as if there was no tomorrow.

"At the next table, I saw a man wearing a dark suit, sitting alone, drinking a bottle of Rhine wine. As I said, the place was packed, but he was the only patron with a table entirely to himself. Herr Froschmeier, who was rude to all his other customers, never missed politely nodding his head when he walked by, without receiving the least acknowledgement in return.

"That man was over 50; he had a full mane of dirty, grey hair; his forehead was unusually large and shiny; his eyes were a very pale blue and rather large and penetrating; his mouth was thin, harsh, with a sense of droopy bitterness accentuated by the heavy Bavarian pipe he was smoking; his chest was powerful, and he had beautifully chiseled hands. If it wasn't for the pallor of his skin, he would have looked like a strong and healthy man.

"He seemed to be looking everywhere and nowhere at once, making his drink last. When he got up to borrow a box of matches from a neighboring table, rather imperiously, I was surprised to discover that he had short legs, as I had expected him to be tall. His walk was, in fact, odd: he waddled on his stubby, knock-kneed legs, and he looked like a strange combination of the torso of an Apollo stuck on the lower appendages of a faun.

"My table-mate, who had noticed my interest, winked at me, nudged me with his elbow, and said:

" 'That's the famous Professor Krausse. They say he's the greatest doctor in all of Germany. He cured the Kaiser when he was sick. They said he bullied him just as he would have done any peasant. He's quite a character!'

"The Professor couldn't have heard what my neighbor had said, but somehow, he noticed that he was being observed. His pale eyes came to rest on me for a few seconds, then he made a gesture to summon the landlord.

"The man came running, almost trampling his customers in his rush to obey, sat respectfully at the Professor's table, exchanged a few words, then came to our table and said:

" 'Herr Professor Krausse requests the two gentlemen's company.'

"I normally don't like being summoned in such a way, and was about to reject the offer, when I caught my companion's anxiety.

" 'From someone like him, such an invitation is an order,' he said, begging me. 'We can't refuse, or there may be trouble for me.'

"So I decided to go along and accept the Professor's invitation; besides, I was curious to meet such a character.

"After sitting at his table, the Professor had two glasses brought and poured some wine into them. Then, he turned towards my companion and said:

" 'Lieutenant Schwalbe, how many times has your gossipy tongue gotten you in trouble and hurt your career?'

"The Guardsman became flushed, then pale, and apologized immediately:

" 'I'm sorry, Herr Professor. I didn't say anything bad about you, as the gentleman will attest. I could only repeat what everyone knows, that you are the greatest doctor in all of Germany...'

" 'And you, Herr Lieutenant, are the greatest ass in all of Germany.' He then ignored the poor officer and fixed his gaze on me. 'You're a foreigner... That's easy to see... An American, but naturalized British... Not difficult to tell, either. You're skilled at deduction, but uncomfortable with relying on your intuition. It's a fault, but it shouldn't prove to be too much of a handicap in your future. I don't know why you're here today, but before the War, I would have recommended to our authorities that someone as dangerous as you be escorted back to the border in haste.'

"I was stunned by his clairvoyance, as well as by his rudeness. I was about to respond when he stopped me with a simple gesture:

" 'No need. I wasn't trying to offend you. Only imbeciles are offended by the truth, and you're no such thing, despite the superficiality of your education.'

"I couldn't help but laugh, but Professor Krausse replied at once:

" 'Your laughter is meaningless; it only masks your lack of a response. I am, in fact, greatly honoring you by declaring you an enemy of Germany. Fortunately, you won't be staying in our country long.'

" 'Why do you persist in seeing me as your enemy?' I asked.

" 'Because you do not truly understand Germany, her spirit, her essence, her potential, her future… Your judgment is impaired on all those points. At any other time in our history, it wouldn't matter at all, but after our defeat, we must learn to take into account the opinions of foreigners like you—for our greatest misery.'

"As I now reflect upon what the Professor told me that night, I realize that he had indeed shared some very perceptive insights with me, but at the time, I only saw it as an amusing conversation.

"We emptied our glasses; the wine was excellent and I found out later that a bottle of it cost 12,000 marks. As I politely took my leave, the Professor said:

" 'Remember the name of this tavern and its proprietor; you'll soon hear more about them. Good night.'

"Several months later, the ghastly truth about the tavern of *Nachtrabengasse* was exposed. Herr Froschmeier was arrested and accused of having served human meat to his customers. A veritable charnel was discovered in his cellars. Froschmeier and several of his accomplices—including Lieutenant Schwalbe, who had helped procure victims by befriending strangers—had their heads cut off."

"What about Professor Krausse?" asked Tom Wills, the detective's new assistant.

"Be patient, Tom. My story is only beginning. I saw him again yesterday."

"You did! Where?"

"Here, in London, in this very Baker Street flat."

CHAPTER ONE
The Second Meeting

Mrs. Crown, Harry Dickson's landlady, let the visitor in. The man, without waiting for an invitation, went to sit in an in armchair in front of the Great Detective.

"I suppose you recognize me, Mr. Dickson?" he said.

Harry Dickson did indeed. Professor Krausse hadn't aged much, despite the fact that ten years had passed since their first meeting. His hair was a little thinner and his shoulders more stooped, a fact which Dickson remarked upon.

"Yes, time is the great enemy of all men," replied the Professor. "Especially for those who don't understand its power, like you, Mr. Dickson. I see a few lines on your forehead now, four gold fillings in your mouth, and you appear to smoke with much less calm than you used to."

"I'll be happy to repay your previous hospitality with a glass of wine," said the detective. "It is the only thing that improves with age."

"Among material things, yes; but no, I would prefer some of your national drink: whiskey. Wine is generally terrible in England."

Harry Dickson offered the Professor a bottle of Black & White and seltzer. The German served himself a small drink.

"I have come to ask you to secure the pardon of a man sentenced to hang," he then said, matter-of-factly.

Dickson was taken aback.

"But I have no power in such matters!"

"Tut, tut!" said the old man. "You have rendered too many services to the Crown of England not to be entitled to ask for such a small favor, especially since we're talking about a vulgar crime and a no less vulgar criminal, with very little importance."

"If so, why are you interested in him?"

"He is one of my mental patients."

"Heavens! That's a rather strange reason."

"Not at all. His cure—which I effected—was the result of a long and difficult series of experiments. But once cured, the man stupidly chose to leave Germany and go and commit a murder in England."

"Who are we talking about?" inquired Dickson.

"His name is Schwertfeger. He's a German sailor. He recently robbed and killed another sailor."

"Ah yes, I recall the case. This Schwertfeger had some nasty antecedents. I believe he'd been sentenced to life in prison in Germany for a double murder, if I recall correctly."

"That's right. I was the one who had that sentence commuted."

"I see. And why do you seek clemency for this villain again?"

"Because if you hang him, he'll die too early."

"I confess I don't, understand, Professor. What do you mean by 'too early?'"

"What I just said: too early—before his time, if you prefer."

"I'm afraid I must ask..."

"...for an explanation? Of course. But there's really very little to tell. After six years inside the Moabit Prison, Schwertfeger's mind had regressed to the point of idiocy. As it happened, I was visiting the infirmary of the prison when I came across his case. I thought it was interesting and asked for permission to experiment on him, which was granted. My experiment was a success and the patient regained all his mental faculties. I then asked that he be remanded in my care for some further tests, which was also granted. Unfortunately, the ingrate escaped, managed to stowaway on a cargo ship en route to England, where he started his new life by murdering a fellow sailor, as you well know.

"I'm here to ask this service of you as a man of science, Mr. Dickson. My experiments might ultimately benefit far worthier men than Schwertfeger, but in order to ascertain that, they must be allowed to run their course."

Harry Dickson considered the Professor's request. His undeniable intelligence and probity naturally pleaded in his favor.

"The most I can secure for your subject," he finally told the Professor, "is his transfer to a lunatic asylum. There, you will be able to observe him at your leisure."

"I can ask for nothing more."

"In that case, I will start working on it at once," said the detective

"I am very grateful. And since one good turn deserves another, I see that you suffer from one of the molars on your upper left jaw. You're planning to have it pulled, no doubt on advice from your dentist. That would be a mistake. You only have a mild case of sinusitis, undetected by your doctor. If you get that taken care of, you will no longer have any problems with your tooth."

Professor Krausse then left without further ado. Curious about his parting diagnosis, Dickson went to visit his doctor the next day. The man scoffed a little at the

Professor's recommendation, but agreed that a sinus drainage could do no harm and performed the task at once. The following night, Dickson noticed that the pain was gone. Professor Krausse had been right!

Harry Dickson had no trouble requesting a new psychiatric evaluation of Schwertfeger. That resulted in the subject's death sentence being commuted and he was speedily transferred to a padded cell at Bedlam.

Two days later, however, Schwertfeger's cell was found empty. The bird had flown the coop. He had miraculously escaped.

That same day, Dickson received a telephone call from Professor Krausse.

"I am very grateful to you, Mister Dickson," said the German doctor.

"I understand, but Schwertfeger's escape has caused me great embarrassment, as you might well guess," replied the detective in a dark mood.

"Indeed, and I apologize for it, but it was easier to engineer his evasion from Bedlam than from Newgate."

"What do you mean—engineer his evasion?"

"Come, Mister Dickson, I won't lie to you. That's why I came here. I need Schwertfeger not inside a cell, but in my laboratory. Good-bye now. I doubt we shall meet again."

The Professor hung up. The detective couldn't find more information about him or his subject, but he wasn't the type of man to back down from a challenge. Many telephone calls were exchanged between Baker Street and Friedrichstrasse, the headquarters of the German police. Soon, Dickson was in possession of some information that left him even more puzzled and aggravated.

Schwertfeger, according to the German police, was never mentally retarded, nor was he found in prison and